RL
AR
Quiz

THE GREAT EGGSPECTATIONS OF LILA FENWICK

THE GREAT EGGSPECTATIONS OF LILA FENWICK

Kate McMullan

Pictures by Diane de Groat

Farrar, Straus and Giroux

New York

*Many thanks to Lee Ann Jones Messer, librarian, and to
Pam Sherman and her class—especially Missy Roedersheimer,
Jenny Nowak, Rebecca Masser, Richard Smith, and
Christopher Erwin Foltz—at the Conococheague Elementary
School in Hagerstown, Maryland, for all of their
eggscellent advice!*

Text copyright © 1991 by Kate McMullan
Pictures copyright © 1991 by Diane de Groat
Library of Congress catalog card number: 90-56152
Published simultaneously in Canada by HarperCollins*CanadaLtd*
Printed in the United States of America
First edition, 1991

For my sixth-grade teacher,

KENNETH E. LACKEY

THE GREAT EGGSPECTATIONS OF LILA FENWICK

SIXTH-GRADE SOMEBODY

As I hurried up Clayton Road, I spotted my best friend waiting for me on the corner, in front of the ice-cream parlor. Good old Gayle. The morning sun at her back turned her wild blond hair into a frizzy halo. As I got closer, I saw that she'd chosen a pair of black jeans and her black *Cats* T-shirt to make her first-day-of-school entrance. I wished I'd worn something a bit flashier than a plain white blouse over old blue jeans, but never mind. I had more important things to think about than my wardrobe.

We started walking toward school, side by side, and I launched into my scheme: "Do me a big favor?"

"Fair friend, thou hast but to name the favor and it is thine." Gayle had not quite recovered from acting in her summer camp's production of *Romeo and Juliet*.

"In that case, would you consider doing all my math homework for me?"

This just got me one of her looks.

"Okay, so here's the real favor. You know how a sixth-grader is always Student Council president?"

She nodded.

"Well, we're sixth-graders now, and it's our turn to run the school. I want you to nominate me."

Gayle's eyebrows went up. "For president?" Then she smiled. "Yeah, I can see you up there, banging the gavel. It's a good idea."

"Not a good idea," I told her. "A Great Idea."

Coming up with Great Ideas is my specialty. Don't take my word for it, ask Gayle. She could tell you how once, on a rainy day, I talked our gym teacher into showing us how to do sixties dances, like the Monkey and the Mashed Potato, instead of square dancing. Or how I started the petition that got rid of beef curry in the school cafeteria once and for all. And what could better qualify a person for being Student Council president than coming up with lots of Great Ideas?

I think Gayle was surprised when I asked her to nominate me, because I've never been ambitious. I've always been content to stay in the background while other kids run the show. If they get stuck or need help with something, they know where to come for a Great Idea. Over the summer, though, I'd done some thinking. Why shouldn't I try to be in charge once in a while? I knew I could do it, be *somebody* this year. Sixth grade was going to be different.

But as we walked up the steps to Price School and into our new classroom, things didn't seem very different. For starters, there behind the sixth-grade teacher's desk was Mr. Sherman, our fifth-grade teacher. He just smiled and said he'd been promoted with us. And I was glad to see that Chocolate, the guinea pig we'd had as class pet last year, had been promoted, too.

Just about everybody in our class seemed the same. Gayle had spent the summer at a "fat camp" and had lost a bunch of pounds, but she'd come home and pudged right back up to her comfortable old self again. Eddie English was still a *total knockout*, Mr. TKO, when it came to looks. Barney Barker's belly still hung down over his belt, and if you looked at him, he'd point to his eye, his head, at you, and then pinch his nose, all the signs for "I-think-you-stink!" Rita Morgan, Miss Perfect, was winding the tip of her ponytail around her finger and blabbing away about her *fabulous* summer and how she'd met this un*real* guy at the mall who loved listening to Shell Shock rock just as much as she did. Kelly MacConnell's face was its usual forest of freckles after her summer on the swim team. Lynn Williamson was sitting quietly by herself as always. Jason Johnson was still picking away at his nose, while Roger Rupp and Tim Petefish clomped little plastic dinosaurs around on their desks and made growling noises. As I took the seat in front of him, Tim burped in my ear and said, "Hi ya, Toothpick Legs." Not much had changed.

Well, maybe a couple of things. I had my new ambition to become Student Council president. Sandra Guth now had railroad-track braces, top and bottom. And my old friend Michael Watson, who used to say he was so skinny he could tread water in a garden hose, had lifted weights over the summer and sprouted a couple of muscles. But that was it.

As the 8:20 bell rang, Mr. Sherman stood up behind his desk. "Class, will you please come to order."

We stopped talking.

"Welcome to sixth grade. I'm happy to see your familiar faces and I hope you're happy to see mine."

We were. Sherman Tank was always fair, and he just seemed to expect us to try our hardest and do our best, and so for him we did.

"Mr. Sherman?" It was Sandra. "Remember at the end of school last year when we gave you *A Tale of Two Cities*?"

"It's right here," Mr. Sherman said, tapping a red-leather book on his desk.

"We thought you'd read it to the new fifth-graders, but now you've got us again."

He nodded. "I've chosen some other books to read to you this year, but I look forward to reading your gift to next year's class."

"Awww! Read it to us again!" said Barney. "I want to hear about those guys getting their heads chopped off!" He drew a finger across his throat and made choking sounds.

"Yeah, we loved that story!" said Eddie. Several of us nodded in agreement.

Mr. Sherman looked pleased. "Well, I suppose I could read you another book by Charles Dickens. Let's see . . . There's one I haven't read in years, but it used to be my favorite. *Great Expectations.*"

"Great what?" asked Barney.

"Expectations are things you expect," said Mr. Sherman. "A person with great expectations expects great things to happen."

"Like the Cardinals winning the Series!" called out Roger.

"Like getting straight A's," said Gayle.

Like being elected Student Council president, I thought . . .

Mr. Sherman nodded. "Now, Mr. English?"

Eddie looked toward the door to our room, to see if his father had walked in, but Mr. Sherman was looking right at him.

"Me?"

"That's right. We will be a bit more formal in the sixth grade."

Chalk up one more difference.

"Can you tell us briefly about your summer, Mr.

English?" But before Mr. English had time to reply, someone did appear at our door. "Oh, come in, Ms. Wong," Mr. Sherman said.

"Is this a good time for me to talk to your class?" she asked. "Or shall I come back later?"

"Now's fine."

Carrying a stack of papers, a beautiful Asian woman walked by our desks to where Mr. Sherman was standing. She wore glasses, just like me. Hers were round, with thick black frames, the kind of glasses the star of an old movie might wear to make her seem intellectual. Then, just as the hero is about to kiss her, he slips off her glasses and . . . surprise! He realizes that she's gorgeous.

"Class," said Mr. Sherman, "Ms. Wong is our new librarian. She's got some projects lined up that I think you'll really enjoy."

"I'm glad to be here," Ms. Wong said. Her glossy straight black hair nearly reached her waist. "I've just moved to St. Louis from Los Angeles, where I was the assistant librarian in a very large school with six classes in each grade level. I couldn't get to know all my students there, but I have a feeling things will be different here at Price School." She smiled, showing white, even teeth. "I've invited some authors to visit us during library period this year and I'll be sponsoring a school newspaper. But first I'd like to start the year off with a little experiment." She gave half the papers she was holding to Eddie and the other half to Sandra. "Will you two please pass these out for me?"

We each got a little stapled-together booklet, sealed with a red-dot sticker on the side.

"These booklets contain the directions for a project that we did in my California school," she told us. "I think it might be fun to try it here, too. Please don't open them yet."

On the front cover, it said: AN EGGSPERIMENT IN RESPONSIBILITY. *Eggs*periment? Right away, I knew I liked Ms. Wong. I'd never understood why correct spelling was such a big deal, and now here was a teacher who obviously felt the same!

"Today," said Ms. Wong, "is a beginning for all of us. It's the beginning of sixth grade for you. It's the beginning of a new job for me. Now, who can answer this question about beginnings: Which came first, the chicken or the egg?"

"The chicken!" Barney Barker yelled. Then he started clucking and flapping his elbows up and down.

"Really?" said Ms. Wong. "But where did the chicken come from?"

Barney scrunched up his face. "The egg?"

Ms. Wong laughed. "Don't worry. No one's ever been able to answer this question. I just wanted to get you started thinking about things, about eggs in particular. Eggs are the beginning of many things."

"Yeah, like rotten eggs!" Barney cracked.

Ms. Wong didn't seem to mind. "Yes, and you, too, started out as an egg."

"In his case, a scrambled egg," Gayle muttered.

I hoped Ms. Wong wasn't going to stand up there and tell us, in the first five minutes of the first day of school, about how babies are made. Luckily, she didn't.

"I'd like you to wait to open your booklets until you're ready to do your homework. Let's see"— she looked over at Mr. Sherman—"today's Wednesday. When does the sixth grade have library?"

"Mondays," said Mr. Sherman.

"All right, the first assignment will be due next Monday. After you've checked out your books, you can take turns showing what you've made and then I'll give you your eggs."

I didn't have the slightest idea what Ms. Wong was talking about, but she didn't offer any further explanation. With another smile, she walked back out our classroom door.

"Eggs?" I whispered to Gayle.

"Unless mine ears deceive me," Gayle whispered back, "she said eggs."

THE EGGSPERIMENT

The rest of the school day whizzed by so fast that we didn't really have a chance to think about Ms. Wong and her mysterious assignment. When the 3:30 bell rang, I stuffed her booklet in my bag, along with my new math and science books.

As Gayle and I headed for the door, Rita called, "Wait for *moi!*" and scurried to catch up with us. "Can you believe all this homework?" she complained. "My book bag weighs a ton!"

Out on the sidewalk, Kelly and Sandra came running up behind us. "Did you guys read that stuff from Ms. Wong yet?" Kelly asked breathlessly.

"Some experiment with eggs?" I said.

"I hope we don't have to do anything with raw eggs," said Rita. "That slimy clear part makes me gag."

Kelly looked at Sandra. "They haven't read it. Stop a sec."

"You won't believe this." Sandra shook her head.

We stepped off the sidewalk and sat down in the shade of a maple tree on the school lawn.

Kelly opened her EGGSPERIMENT IN RESPONSIBIL- ITY booklet. " 'Congratulations!' " she read. " 'You are about to become parents!' "

"Let me see that!" Gayle grabbed the booklet from Kelly. " 'Dear Students: Congratulations! You are about to become parents!' "

Kelly snatched the booklet back and continued. " 'Your child happens to be a hard-boiled egg. Nevertheless, you are totally responsible for this child. You must care for it and provide for all its needs.' "

"Is this a joke?" I asked.

" 'This is an experiment to see how it feels to handle a big responsibility,' " Kelly read on. " 'You will also be learning to use the library's reference materials, writing books of your own, and using your creative thinking ability and common sense. All the assignments must be completed and your child must survive in order for this eggsperiment to be successful. Good luck in this adventure! I am sure that you can do it. Sincerely, your new li- brarian, Ms. Wong.' "

Kelly looked up wide-eyed.

"We're getting egg-babies?" I asked.

"What do eggs, like, have to do with library anyway?" Rita demanded.

Kelly shrugged. "Search me."

"At least it sounds more interesting than memorizing the Dewey decimal system," said Gayle.

"The Dewey who-y?" asked Rita.

"Ms. Wong's okay," I said. "She didn't let Barney get on her nerves."

"Listen to the first assignment." Kelly started reading again. " 'BUILD. An egg-baby must be cared for in a safe place. Your egg-baby will also have to be transported to and from school inside its home. Build a safe, easy-to-carry environment for your egg-baby.' "

"That's it?" asked Rita. "Doesn't she say how to make it?"

Kelly shook her head. "That's all it says."

"This is *totally* confusing." Rita stood up. "I'm asking Mr. Sherman about it tomorrow."

She marched off and the rest of us walked home together. As we'd planned, Gayle came home with me. My mom had started to work full-time a couple of weeks before, and while I didn't really mind staying by myself during the day, I wasn't too wild about the idea of walking into an empty house alone.

We'd decided to get to work right away on our egg-baby homes, but our plans were changed by a note on the refrigerator.

Dear Lila,

    I was running late this morning and didn't get a chance to do any laundry. Would you mind putting a load or two in the machine? That would be a big help! I'll scare up something for dinner when I get home.

                                      Mom

"Oh, great!" I crumpled the note into a ball and threw it into the trash. "I hate housework!"

"Not too wild about it myself." Gayle began rooting around in our fridge while I stomped down to the basement to attack the laundry pile that my dad had begun referring to as the Matterhorn.

When I got back to the kitchen, Gayle had not only toasted us a couple of bagels and spread them with cream cheese, just the way my mom used to do when I'd come home from school, but she'd also put some ground beef into a mixing bowl.

"What's that for?"

"Dost thou not wish to sup this very night upon a meat loaf?" She emptied what was left in a package of bread crumbs into the bowl.

"You're making meat loaf?"

Gayle nodded and cracked an egg into the bowl. She stirred it into the meat and bread crumbs, making a sort of slimy paste, and then started chopping up an onion.

"Want me to look up a recipe for you?" I said. "My mom's got hundreds of cookbooks from the B.C. days."

"B.C.?"

"Before Clinic," I translated.

"No, thanks." Now Gayle started cutting up some celery. "With meat loaf, one can improvise!" she explained.

I sat down at the counter to watch. Gayle sure seemed to know what she was doing. "Why'd my mom have to take that stupid job, anyway?"

"Being a physical therapist isn't so stupid."

"She's only a physical therapist's assistant." I watched Gayle survey the little jars in the door of the refrigerator. "Plus, she gets all involved and worried about the patients and their problems, and she's—I don't know—she just doesn't seem to pay attention to things around here anymore."

"It could be worse," Gayle said, adding a dash of Tabasco and a dab of mustard to her creation and then pouring some ketchup into a loaf pan. "When I get home, my mom grills me about every detail of my day—what I learned at school, what we had for lunch, who said what at recess. It drives me bananas. There!" She patted her mixture into the loaf pan and set it in the refrigerator. "Put it in a 350° oven for an hour," she said as she washed her hands. "Now let's go figure out this egg business."

"You know," I said, picking up my book bag, "once you get into it, cooking's not all that bad!"

Upstairs, Gayle plopped down next to me on my bed. "Okay, what would make a good egg-baby environment?"

"A shoe box would work." I went to search my mom's closet and found two. I gave one to Gayle and then looked at the one in my lap with disappointment. "But everybody will use a shoe box."

"So? That doesn't matter."

Maybe not to Gayle, but it did to me. I just had to come up with a Great Idea for an unusual egg-baby home.

While I was thinking, Gayle got to work. She turned her shoe box on its side and, with a ball-point pen, drew flowered wallpaper on all three walls. She penned stripes on the floor for a rug, and added three loops on the ceiling for a light fixture. Then she made a bed by stuffing some Styrofoam peanuts into one of my old socks. I helped her sew on straps that would keep her egg-baby in place, and then went downstairs for an egg so that we could make the straps fit. As I was on my way to the kitchen, the phone rang.

"Hey, Fenwick."

"Hey, Michael." No one else called me Fenwick. "What do you think of Ms. Wong and this egg thing?"

"Eggsasperating," he said. "I've just searched through all our junk and couldn't find everything I need to build that environment. Could I come over and check out your basement?"

"Michael Watson, are you saying our basement's full of junk?"

"How about 'potentially recyclable objects'?"

"That's better. I'm sure it's okay. Come over tomorrow."

"Thanks, Fenwick. *Reservoir.*"

I took an egg from the fridge and went back upstairs.

"Michael just called," I said, handing Gayle the egg.

"Michael?" She fumbled the egg and it rolled onto the floor. Luckily, my pajamas were there to break its fall.

"Yeah." I picked up the egg and put it into the little beanbag bed. "Perfect size."

"So what did he say?"

I cut the straps to the right length and started sewing a snap to one end. "He's coming over to see if he can find some stuff in our basement to use for his egg environment."

"Now?" Gayle sat straight up.

"Take it easy," I told her. "Tomorrow. Why? What's the big deal?"

"Nothing, nothing, nothing." Gayle acted as if it took total concentration to glue the bed to the back wall of her bedroom, but that just made me wonder all the more why she'd acted so weird when Michael's name came up. In a few minutes, she held up her shoe box. "Done!"

"That's it? Aren't you going to put in anything else? It's supposed to be an environment, not just a bed."

"Maybe." She got up to go home. "If I think of anything."

Sometimes, I thought as I walked her to the door, sometimes I wish I could do things as simply and easily as Gayle. She'd spent an hour, tops, on her egg house. And now she was finished. Sometimes having to wait for a Great Idea to strike can be very frustrating.

"I thought I was hallucinating when I walked in the door and smelled dinner cooking!" exclaimed my mother as we sat down at the table that night.

My father looked suspiciously at his plate as if he wasn't exactly wild to be the guinea pig testing my first cooking experiment. But he bravely took a bite and then said, "It's just like the kind we used to cook over an open fire at Camp Ironvale!" That's his ultimate compliment. "What's your secret ingredient?"

"I guess you could say a little pinch of Gayle."

"Oh, Gayle made this?" My mom laughed. "She's getting to be quite the chef, isn't she?"

I wanted to say how I'd watched her, and that making a meat loaf didn't seem like such a big deal to me, but I had a mouth full of meat loaf, and by the time I'd swallowed, my dad had asked my mom how things were going at the clinic.

"I started working with a new patient today," she said. "A boy about your age, Lila."

"You work with kids?" I asked.

"Anyone can get hurt and need physical therapy."

"Maybe I know him. What's his name?"

"That's confidential."

"Why?"

"Patients have a right to privacy when they come to the clinic."

"Well, what's wrong with him?"

"He was fooling around with cherry bombs over the Fourth of July and one went off in his hand."

"The poor kid!"

My mom nodded. "He lost the thumb and forefinger on his right hand, and he's right-handed. When I encouraged him to use his left hand, he tried, but when I asked him to do something with his right, he wouldn't. He's pretty depressed."

My parents went on talking about other things that were happening at the clinic, but I kept thinking about that boy. Would he be able to learn to write a new way? Or hold a baseball bat? He must wish more than anything that he could turn back the clock and relive the Fourth of July, only differently this time, with no cherry bombs. But going back in time happened only in sci-fi books and movies. He was a real kid and for the rest of his real life he was going to have to live without the thumb and first finger on his right hand.

LILA FOR PRESIDENT!

The next morning's class meeting was far from calm and orderly.

"Hey, Brace Face!" Barney Barker called out. "What's with this egg stuff?"

Sandra flashed a metal-mouth grimace. "Did I call on you, Barney?" The day before, she'd been elected chairperson to run the daily meetings that Mr. Sherman thought gave us good experience in democracy.

"But I don't get it!" Barney bellowed.

"Me neither!" yelled Roger.

"I don't want to be a parent of any old egg!" shouted Tim.

"Cut it out, guys!" Sandra had volume on her

side. She waited until everyone was properly quiet and then called on Rita, who'd been sitting primly with her hand up.

"Well, personally," Rita began, "I thought we came to school to, like, learn reading and math, and I don't see why that new librarian is giving us extra work to do, with all this making a home for eggs, and what does it have to do with library, anyway?"

Sandra shrugged and turned to Mr. Sherman. "I think this question's for you."

Mr. Sherman stood up behind his desk. "Ms. Morgan, you're right. You are here at school to learn reading and math, and Ms. Wong's experiment has to do with thinking skills and responsibility. But unless you learn how to think clearly and act responsibly, reading and math don't mean very much."

Rita did not look convinced.

"As far as what the eggsperiment has to do with the library," Mr. Sherman went on, "you'll be using reference books for several of the assignments, as well as writing books of your own."

"But what are we supposed to build?" asked Kelly. "What kind of house does an egg need?"

"As I understand it, you'll be carrying your eggs to and from school, so you'll need to design homes for them that are easy to transport and that will hold the eggs securely so they won't drop and break. Any further questions about the eggs?" When no one raised a hand, he added, "Talking about responsibility reminds me that the elections for Student Council offices are coming up."

"Me for president!" sang out Barney.

"This morning," Mr. Sherman went on, "would be a good time for you to nominate as many students as you wish for each office, and vote on them. We'll need three sixth-grade candidates to run against three fifth-graders for secretary, treasurer, and vice president, and two sixth-grade candidates to run for president. The winners of the class vote will take part in a school-wide election." Mr. Sherman looked around in a way that made me sit up taller in my desk. Then he nodded to Sandra. "Ms. Guth, why don't you call for nominations?"

My heart was beating fast. I looked over at Gayle and she flipped me a thumbs-up.

"Nominations are open for Student Council president." Sandra surveyed the raised hands around the room.

Call on Gayle, I silently coached her.

"Kelly?"

"I nominate Gayle Deckert," said Kelly, and Sandra wrote Gayle's name on the board.

Gayle looked just as surprised as I felt. She slowly lowered her hand. Then suddenly it shot up again. When Sandra called on her, she said, "I decline the nomination."

Good old Gayle, I thought. *A true friend.*

"Ms. Deckert?" It was Mr. Sherman. "Being nominated for the office of Student Council president is a great honor. Obviously, one of your classmates feels that you are the best qualified to hold this office. Out of respect for Ms. MacConnell's opinion, I recommend that you stay in the race."

Gayle looked over and gave me a shrug, as if to say, "Sorry!"

Well, she wasn't half as sorry as I was, but I wasn't giving up without a fight!

As Michael nominated Eddie, I looked desperately around the room and caught Rita's eye.

"Reeeta," I mouthed. "Nominate meeee."

Rita favored me with one of her famous smiles.

"Nom-in-ate meeee!" I mouthed again, pointing first to myself and then to the growing list of names Sandra was writing on the board.

Rita looked at me and then over at the names. Ever so slowly, an expression of awareness dawned. She gave an "Oh, I get it!" nod and raised her hand.

I sighed with relief.

"Rita?" said Sandra.

"I move that nominations cease."

No, no! I shook my head.

"Is there a second?" asked Sandra.

"I second the motion," said Jason.

"All in favor?"

Every sixth-grader but one raised a hand.

"Opposed?"

No hand went up. Not even mine. How could I vote when my greatest expectation for a super sixth-grade year had just been shattered like a raw egg dropped on my head? Splat!

I had hoped I wouldn't get nominated for vice president, secretary, or treasurer, and I didn't. Those offices were about as important as drinking-fountain monitor. It was only the president who had the power and the glory. Número uno.

Mr. Sherman passed out little slips of paper then and we voted for one person for each office. Angry at fate, I voted for our class guinea pig for president. But then I erased Chocolate's name and loyally penciled in Gayle's. Sandra and Mr. Sherman counted the ballots, and right before lunch, Mr. Sherman wrote the dreadful results on the board:

NOMINEES FOR PRESIDENT:	Gayle Deckert
	Eddie English
NOMINEE FOR VICE PRESIDENT:	Kelly MacConnell
NOMINEE FOR TREASURER:	Tim Petefish
NOMINEE FOR SECRETARY:	Rita Morgan

And that was that.

At recess, a mournful Gayle came up to me. "I'm sorry about the way things turned out, Lila."

I shrugged

Rita wasn't far behind Gayle. "I couldn't tell what you were trying to say to me for the longest time!" she declared.

"I gathered."

"Finally I figured out that you didn't want anyone else to get nominated for president, so Gayle would win!" Rita winked at me. "Isn't it unreal that I'm up for secretary?"

"Unreal."

Rita turned to Gayle. "The bad news is that you're running against Eddie. All the boys will vote for him, 'cause, you know, boys always vote for boys, and all the girls will vote for him, too, 'cause he's totally TKO."

"True," said Gayle. "Plus he was vice president last year, so he's got experience."

"Hey! Wait a second!" I said. "It sounds like you're giving up the election before the campaign's even started."

"So?"

"But you can't!"

"Why not? I'll stick up a few posters and make a speech, but why go all out for a losing battle?"

"Gayle's right," said Rita. "Why bother?"

I put my hands on my hips. In my book, giving up was the worst thing anyone could do. I'd just about been guilty of it myself when I didn't get nominated, but now I was back in the race. Okay, so it wasn't going to be me up there with the gavel in my hand. But I was going to work my hardest to make sure that it *was* my best friend.

"Gayle Deckert, you are going to win this election."

"How?" asked Rita. "Are you going to rig the voting?"

I didn't bother to answer.

"Lila, I don't like the look on your face," said Gayle.

"Uh-oh!" Rita said, backing away. "I'm getting out of here before the Great Idea strikes!"

"We have to get organized." I stared at Gayle almost without seeing her. "If we can get the class lists and see how many girls and how many boys there are in the school, then we'll know if it'll work."

"If what'll work?'" Gayle looked confused.

"Operation Girl Power," I told her. "You do want me to be your campaign manager, don't you?"

"I hadn't really thought about it."

"With me in charge, you'll be running this school."

"Okay, okay," said Gayle. "You're hired."

HOME, SWEET HOME

For the next few nights, I went to sleep hoping to dream up a Great Idea for my egg-baby's home. But dreaming didn't provide me with an answer. It wasn't until Sunday afternoon, just twenty-four hours before the project was due, that the Great Idea hatched.

I was helping clean out our hall closet when it happened. Since I had run out of underwear again, I thought doing a few loads of laundry was more urgent, but my mom wanted to donate some of the things we didn't use anymore to a Trash 'n' Treasure sale that was benefitting her clinic, so we were doing closets. I'd already put a pair of roller skates, a small purple backpack I'd used in the pre-homework years, a tattered Cardinals baseball cap, and a flower-pressing kit into the T 'n' T pile. Then, in a big cardboard box stuck way in the back of the closet, I found lots of my old toys, and right down near the bottom was my once favorite doll.

"Singing Deer! I thought you were lost forever!"

"See the benefits of cleaning out closets?" my mom said as she sorted through old coats and jackets next to me.

My dad had brought the little American Indian doll back from a convention out West. He'd told me her name was Singing Deer and I thought it was such a beautiful name that I insisted, for the next few weeks, that my parents call me Singing Deer, too. The doll wore a fringed buckskin dress and leggings. She had on teeny shell earrings and blue moccasins. But what caught my eye this day was the beautiful beaded cradleboard in which she carried her baby, whom I'd named Little Chipmunk. One look at Little Chipmunk, snug on her mother's back, and I knew *eggsactly* what I was going to do for my egg-baby home!

On Monday morning, everyone slunk into the classroom and stuck the little boxes and bundles they carried into their lockers. No one seemed too sure about how the egg-baby environments were supposed to look. We were all half afraid that we might have made ours wrong, so we kept them out of sight.

Except for Rita. She sauntered into the classroom

with a huge, flat-bottomed wicker basket over her arm. If she'd been wearing a cape, she would have looked just like Little Red Riding Hood, taking a big basketful of goodies to Grandma. But even Rita had some inhibitions about showing off her egg-baby home. She'd covered the basket with what had to have been one of her own pink, ruffled baby blankets.

"Any new business?" asked Sandra after she'd called the meeting to order.

Michael announced that Student Council elections would be held on Friday, September 21. Looking at Mr. Sherman's wall calendar, I figured this gave us less than two weeks to get Operation Girl Power going.

No one had any more business, so the meeting was adjourned, and for the rest of the morning we all worked to figure out how cells divided in science, how numbers divided in math, and how syllables divided in language arts.

After lunch, Mr. Sherman started reading us *Great Expectations*. The story's about Pip, an orphan, who lives with his nasty older sister and her kind blacksmith husband, Joe. In the first chapter, Pip is walking through a foggy graveyard when this escaped convict wearing a leg iron grabs him and says he's going to rip out his heart and his liver and roast them and eat them if he doesn't bring him some food and a file. I was so caught up in Pip's problems that it took me by surprise when Mr. Sherman closed the book and said,

"Reading time's up. Please get what you need and walk quietly to the library."

Ms. Wong stood outside the library door. "This looks very mysterious," she said to Michael, who was carrying a big brown paper bag. "A handle's a practical idea," she said, looking at Lynn Williamson's box.

"Oh, my!" she said as Rita walked past with the enormous basket on her arm.

After we had all traipsed in, Ms. Wong asked us to put our egg-baby homes on the long library table while we selected our books. As sixth-graders, we were allowed to take out three at a time, and she suggested that we might be interested in some of the books in the 649 non-fiction section.

After I found the fourth in the *Anne of Green Gables* series, Gayle and I went to investigate the 649s. She read out a couple of titles. "*What Every Baby-Sitter Should Know, Feed Me! I'm Yours!* These books are all about taking care of babies."

"Maybe we'll need them for the eggs," I suggested.

We both took one, just in case, and got in the checkout line behind Michael. I had to laugh when I saw his stack of books: *Interstellar Pig*, *The Robots of Dawn*, and *Our Brand-New Baby*! But Gayle informed me with a straight face that she thought someday Michael would make an excellent father.

Next, Ms. Wong gathered us around the table. "Who'd like to go first?" She pointed at Rita, who was waving her hand. "Please tell me your names as I call on you, to help me learn them."

"Rita Marie Morgan," Rita announced as she stood up and whisked the blanket off her basket. Inside was all sorts of plastic dollhouse furniture, including cribs, high chairs, and changing tables. It didn't seem exactly fair to me that she'd just gone out and bought everything for her egg-baby's room.

At first Ms. Wong just stared at Rita's huge environment. Then she managed to say, "This is very . . . elaborate, Rita, but do you think its size will make it awkward to carry?"

"No problem," replied Rita, picking the basket up by its handle, which was wound in wide pink-and-blue velvet ribbons.

Next, Ms. Wong pointed to Gayle and she showed her shoe-box home, which was exactly the way it had been when she'd left my house after the first day of school.

"Those straps on the bed show good thinking," said Ms. Wong. "You were considering the safety of your child."

For some reason, Gayle's face turned beet red when Ms. Wong referred to her "child."

One by one, we showed our homes. Sandra's shoe-box bedroom was equipped with a trampoline. Kelly had made a little TV set for her baby out of a box that a bar of soap had come in, plus a teeny tiny remote-control beeper so her egg-baby could change channels from its crib! Eddie had wallpapered his shoe box with baseball cards. Jason had forgotten to make an egg home, but he promised to bring one in by next Monday. Not only had Barney not forgotten to do the assignment but his was pretty cool. It was an egg carton, and each little compartment had a purpose: one, lined with flannel, was a bed; one, painted white, was a bathtub; another had toothpicks stuck all around it and Barney explained that it was a playpen. Lynn had made her egg environment in a cigar box. It reminded me of Arrietty's bedroom in *The Borrowers*. She'd even used empty thread spools for the legs of her baby's bed. Roger and Tim held up identical shoe boxes filled with crude construction-paper palm trees and little plastic dinosaurs.

"Do you think dinosaurs might scare a baby?" asked Ms. Wong.

"Naaa," Tim said. "Babies love dinosaurs."

Next, Ms. Wong pointed to Michael.

"Michael Watson," he said as he reached into his paper bag. What he pulled out was definitely not a shoe box. His bike helmet appeared first, followed by a cantaloupe-sized Styrofoam ball that I recognized as coming from my mom's big box labeled MISCELLANEOUS. Michael had cut in little windows, put a cardboard rim around the middle, and painted the whole thing silver so it looked like a spaceship! Shiny metal bolt ends and wires poked out every which way.

We all stared as Michael released three hooks from three eyes under the rim, and twisted the

ball open. He'd hollowed out the inside and on the bottom half had screwed cup hooks into the thick Styrofoam, anchoring them with flat washers and nuts. Heavy rubber bands stretched between the hooks.

"See," explained Michael, "the egg fits here, in the middle. The rubber bands will hold the egg and suspend it so that it's not touching anything else, and if it gets bumped, it'll move but it won't break."

Michael closed his spaceship and fastened the hooks. At the bottom, a spring stuck out, and now he attached it and four wires from the rim to his bike helmet. Then he put the helmet on, snapping the straps under his chin. The spaceship sat at an angle on top of his head. "Portability," he said, turning to give us all a good view.

Ms. Wong's eyes were wide behind her glasses. "I think we have an inventor here!"

"He's a genius," Rita whispered to me. "An honest-to-goodness certifiable genius."

"Anyone else?" asked Ms. Wong.

Why had I waited till last? My idea was original, too, but now, next to Michael's, how could it look anything but ordinary?

"Lila Fenwick," I said as I stood up, holding my old purple backpack.

"Ah," said Ms. Wong, when she saw it, "someone else thought about portability."

I unzipped the flap and pulled it down. I'd filled the bottom of the pack with pillow stuffing, and sewed a piece from an old quilt on top of it, in case my egg-baby ever took a great fall. Then I'd cut two more pieces from the quilt to line the back and flap of my pack and stitched them around the edges, leaving little openings at the top so I could poke in more pillow stuffing. When the linings were nice and plump, I'd sewed the openings closed. Then, on the inside of the pack, I'd made a snug pouch for my egg-baby to sit in. The home seemed safe, but boring, so I'd made a little mobile out of wire, yarn, glue, and animal crackers. Its main wire was wound around a large paper clip. Now, when I opened the pack, I slipped the paper clip over the folded-back part of the flap near the zipper, and the little cookie lion, tiger, and elephant dangled tantalizingly above the egg-baby's seat for a few seconds before toppling over.

Ms. Wong just smiled. "Nice try. Interesting toys do help to stimulate a baby's mental development."

"I've got one more thing." Reaching into my pocket, I pulled out a tiny teddy bear, just an inch tall. Everyone oooh'ed and aaah'ed when they saw it.

Then Ms. Wong looked around the room. "I think you're ready now." We were quiet, watching, as she went to her desk, pulled open the big bottom drawer, and took out two egg cartons. She came back to where we were sitting and opened them. Inside were bright white eggs, not-quite-so-white eggs, beige eggs with an almost pinkish tinge, and lovely deep brown eggs. She passed in front of us and we each picked out our egg-baby.

When it was her turn, Rita stood up and whispered something in Ms. Wong's ear. "Well, it's an interesting idea, Rita," the librarian said, "but have you considered the extra work it would mean?"

"I've thought about it," Rita said as she looked at the eggs Ms. Wong held out to her for what seemed like a long time. Finally, she plucked a white egg from one carton—and then reached into the second carton and took out another white egg. "Twins," she announced proudly.

When my turn came, I picked one of the pinky-beige eggs. I cupped it between my palms, feeling how warm and smooth and somehow satisfying it was to hold. I know this sounds crazy, but I felt sort of attached to my egg-baby right from the start.

After she passed out the eggs, Ms. Wong gave each of us a spiral-bound notebook filled with heavy blank pages. She said that these were our Egg-Baby Books, and that Assignment 4 was to write in them about our egg-babies every day.

"Hey, what's this?" Barney held up his egg and pointed to a small purple rubber-stamped squiggle on the bottom of the big end.

"That's the official egg-baby birthmark," Ms. Wong explained. "These egg-babies aren't just any old hard-boiled eggs, you know."

"I get it," said Michael. "They're marked so that if an egg breaks we can't just boil up a replacement."

Ms. Wong nodded. "Now, here are the rules for taking care of your egg-babies. You must keep them with you at all times, unless you can find a qualified person to baby-sit."

Lynn raised her hand. "I sit for the little boy next door. Would that qualify me to baby-sit for someone's egg?"

Ms. Wong shook her head. "You may take care of one another's eggs only if you pass my baby-sitter's quiz, but you may ask an adult to sit, or someone with sitting experience who is not involved in the eggsperiment." Ms. Wong could tell that we were confused. "You see, one purpose of the eggsperiment is to give you a feeling of what an enormous responsibility a baby is. I don't want to make it too easy for you to pass that responsibility on to another person."

"But if we're supposed to be the parents of these eggs," objected Gayle, "wouldn't we automatically qualify as sitters?"

"A good point," said Ms. Wong. "When people become parents, it means that they have the responsibility for taking care of children, but it doesn't necessarily mean that they're good at it. Now, I hope it won't happen, but if any of you should drop your egg and crack it, bring it to me, Dr. Wong, here at the Library Hospital, and we'll figure out how seriously injured your child is."

"What happens if our eggs get, like, really squished?" asked Rita.

Ms. Wong held her palms up. "No more egg-baby."

"And we're out of the eggsperiment?" asked Eddie.

Ms. Wong nodded. "Now, I'd like you to do Assignments 2 and 3 and start on 4 by next Monday. For those of you who complete all the assignments and whose egg-babies survive the whole time, Mr. Sherman has come up with a wonderful follow-up activity."

"You mean a reward?" asked Roger.

"You could call it that."

"What? What?" We all wanted to know.

"It's a secret for now, but I'll tell you this: the activity will take place on Saturday, September 29."

"That's when the Fall Festival is," said Sandra.

Ms. Wong just smiled.

"Shell Shock's playing that night!" Rita squealed.

"Yeah," Kelly sighed, "but tickets have been sold out for about a year."

"So?" said Eddie. "It's an outdoor concert. Anybody can just sit on the grass and hear it."

"You can hear it," said Sandra, "but unless you have a seat, you won't be able to see anything. You might as well stay home and listen to it on the radio."

"And to get a seat, like, really close to the stage," moaned Rita, "you need a *ticket*."

FIRST-GRADE FLAK

Walking next to Gayle down the hall to our class-room, I felt different from the way I'd felt walking to the library. Inside my pack was an egg-baby that was all mine to take care of.

Rita was in front of us, yakking away to Michael. "But how did you ever think of it?" She blinked up at the bizarre contraption on his head. "I *never* could have thought of that in a billion light-years."

Michael shrugged. "I read an article once about this contest to see if anyone could invent packaging that would protect a raw egg if it were dropped off the top of a four-story building. The only one that worked had the egg suspended with rubber bands inside a big cylinder, so I thought I'd try something similar."

"That is *so* intelligent of you. I got my idea from looking at catalogues of baby furniture. I wanted everything to, you know, match? But I couldn't decide if I was going to have a boy egg and use blue for my color scheme, or a girl and use pink, and that's when I got the idea of twins."

Gayle poked me and we waited for Michael to tell Rita what a dumb idea it was to have two eggs because it would be double the trouble, but to our surprise, he just said, "Yeah, nobody else even thought about twins."

Gayle rolled her eyes, but I'd spotted something that made me lose interest in Rita's flirting techniques. On the wall right outside the sixth-grade classroom, an orange poster had been taped up: EDDIE ENGLISH FOR PRESIDENT!

"Guess the campaign's started," Gayle said.

"But," I reminded her, "it's a long way from over."

Gayle sat on the bottom rung of the jungle gym at recess, holding her shoe box on her lap. I sat one bar above her, wearing my egg-baby pack and studying copies of the class lists that I'd talked Mrs. Goldstein, the school receptionist, into giving me.

"What's the count so far?" asked Gayle.

"It's pretty close, but I'm only up to the third grade. It's got twelve boys and thirteen girls, so that's one more for us." I put a tally mark in my

GIRLS column and started counting the fourth-grade class. I worked on in silence. At last I held up my tally sheet. "Operation Girl Power it is!"

"Let's see." Gayle peered over my shoulder. "Lila! Are these tally marks right?"

"Okay, it's a narrow margin."

"*Three* more girls than boys in the whole school! I'll say it's narrow."

"Three girls equals three votes," I told Gayle with assurance as I slid off my jungle-gym perch. I was about to suggest some vote-getting, when I saw Rita burst out the front door of the school and come flying down the steps toward us, her egg basket swinging wildly on her arm.

"Lila! Gayle!" she cried. "This is unbelievable!"

"What?" said Gayle.

"Guess what I found in Mr. Sherman's desk drawer!"

"What were you doing snooping in his desk?" I asked.

Breathlessly, Rita started in. "I pinched my thumb on the swing chain and was on my way to the nurse's office when I remembered that Mr. Sherman always used to keep a box of Band-Aids in his drawer, so I went into our room, and Mr. Sherman wasn't there, but I didn't think he'd mind if I helped myself to a Band-Aid, so I opened up his drawer"—she grabbed my arm—"and guess what was there?"

"All your bottles of nail polish that he's confiscated?" I said.

"Tickets!" she squeaked. "A whole pack of tickets for the Shell Shock concert!"

"You're kidding!" Gayle said. "I never pictured Mr. Sherman as the Shell Shock type."

"Don't you get it?" Rita's wide blue eyes flicked from Gayle to me. "This is what Ms. Wong was talking about! The tickets—they're, like, our reward for not cracking up our eggs!"

"Hey, that'd be so cool!" Gayle bent back into a limbo posture and started strumming crazily on her shoe box, imitating Oggie, the lead Shell Shock singer, on his guitar.

"You really think the tickets are for us?" I asked.

"Who else could they be for?" Rita loosened her grip on my arm. "I've got to spread the word!" She took off for the lower field.

Gayle peeked inside her shoe box to make sure the Oggie imitation hadn't damaged her egg. "If Rita's right, that's pretty strong incentive for taking care of these babies."

Just then Ms. Houghton's first-grade class came down the steps for recess. "Hey!" I said. "Time to do a little campaigning."

"Lila, I don't think—"

But I was already jogging over to the big oak just outside the lower-school door. "Girls! First-grade girls! Come here for a second!"

Shyly, the little girls came over to me. I knew how they felt. When I was in first grade, if a big sixth-grader had taken the time to talk to me, I would have been truly honored.

"Listen," I said, stooping down to be at their eye level, "do any of you know what the Student Council is?"

"Yeth!" said a girl with both front teeth missing.

A few of the others nodded yes, but most shook their heads no.

"Well, Student Council's like the government of the school. And now you're not little kindergartners anymore, you're big first-graders, so you get to vote for who will be president."

"My daddy says I'm not old enough to vote for President," said a girl with brown pigtails.

This was going to be harder than I thought.

"Not for President of the United States, but you are old enough to vote for president of the Price School Student Council." I pointed to Gayle. "This is Gayle Deckert. She's running for president."

Gayle gave her best politician's smile.

"Can you say her name?" I asked.

"Gay-ell Deck-ert!" they chanted.

"Very good! Now, it's really important to remember *Gayle's* name so you can vote for *Gayle*. Her name starts with the letter *G*." I picked up a stick from the ground and traced a big capital *G* in the dirt.

"Tho doeth my name," spluttered the little girl with the missing teeth. "But I'm not voting for her."

"You . . . you're not?" I said. "But why? We girls have to stick together. That way we'll have Girl Power!"

"I'm voting for Eddie," said the little girl. "He'th my couthin."

"Your cousin," I repeated, straightening up.

"I'm voting for Gloria's cousin, too," said the pigtailed girl.

"Me, too," said a couple of the others.

"Race you to the swings!" called one of the turncoats, and then they all took off running.

"Just remember," I called after my scattering audience, "a vote for Gayle is a vote for Girl Power!"

Gayle stood there by the tree, drumming her fingers on her shoe box and glaring at me. "Seems that Operation Girl Power is not one of your best Great Ideas, Lila."

"Maybe not," I admitted. "But don't worry! There's still plenty of time for me to come up with another one."

"That," she said, "is what worries me."

BERTHA VAN EGG

Even though Easter was more than six months away, I was hosting an egg-decorating party. Gayle, Kelly, Sandra, and Rita had come over to my house so that we could work together on Assignment 2, which was to draw faces on our eggs and make their birth certificates. We were sitting around the kitchen table, where I'd put out colored pencils, markers, glue, glitter, cotton balls, pipe cleaners, yarn, scraps of material, and my sewing kit.

"Pass the blue marker," said Rita. "*Merci.* Here are some eyes for you, Jennifer," she crooned as she drew enormous blue circles on one of her eggs. Then she took the black marker and added long,

curving eyelashes. "And eyes for you, Jonathan."
Rita gave Jonathan the same big blue eyes, but
shorter, straight eyelashes, as she hummed a few
bars from a Shell Shock hit, "I Can't Keep Up with
You, Baby!" She sighed. "Which one do you think
is the most TKO?"

"Of our eggs?" asked Sandra.

"Of Shell Shock," said Rita. "Oggie is for sure
the cutest, but when Boris starts banging his head
on that Chinese gong, I about think I'm going to
die!"

Kelly held up her egg. "What should I name
her?"

"How about Rochelle?" I suggested.

Kelly laughed. "*Rochelle!* That's a perfect name
for an egg!"

"Rochelle's beautiful," said Sandra.

We all agreed. Kelly was a whiz with a marker.
She'd made Rochelle look like a real baby somehow, with pudgy pink cheeks, rosebud lips, and
one little curl of hair on the top of her head.

"Here's Albert Einstein," said Gayle. "The
world's most brilliant egg."

"That ought to be the name of Michael's egg,"
said Rita. "He is so geniusy plus totally TKO."

Gayle scowled at Rita and then held her egg at
arm's length to get a good look. Done hurriedly
in black marker, it had eyes, a nose, a mouth, wild
scribble hair, and two biggish ears. "Think he looks
like Einstein?"

"Didn't Einstein have a mustache?" I asked.

"Not when he was a baby!" said Kelly.

Gayle drew a bushy mustache on her egg. "I'm done." She stuck Albert in the nearest egg carton and stood up. "I shall see what beckons now from yonder fridge."

"How do you like Natasha?" asked Sandra, holding up the dark-haired, brown-eyed egg that she'd named for some star gymnast on the Russian Olympic team. Sandra had given her a wide smile and a mouth full of braces to match her own. "Watch. She does a great forward somersault." With that, Sandra rolled Natasha, barely managing to grab her before she plunged off the side of the table. "Yow!" she said. "Close call."

I finished gluing brown yarn onto my egg's head and held her up for a final inspection. "Everyone, meet Bertha."

"Howdy, Bertha," said Kelly.

"Her full name's Bertha van Egg," I told them. "Get the yolk?"

For a few seconds, everyone stared blankly at me, until Gayle groaned. "I get it!" she called from behind the refrigerator door. "Birth-of-an-egg!"

Then everyone groaned.

"Don't let them bother you," I told Bertha as I tucked her into her little seat in the backpack. "Van Egg is a very old and respectable name. Your fore-chickens probably came over on the *Mayflower* . . . or should I say May-*fowl*-er?"

Gayle stuck a pitcher under the ice maker and the clanking of cubes drowned out the next round of groans.

I started working on Bertha's birth certificate. First I wrote her name and under MOTHER I wrote mine. It took me a while to figure out how I could make fingerprints and footprints for an egg. Across from me, Sandra was experimenting with putting some backspin on Natasha's somersault.

"Ta-dah!" Gayle came to the table, carrying a tray with five glasses, a pitcher filled with an icy drink, and a plate of nachos. "The green pepper ones are hot," she warned.

We all dug in.

"Mmmmmm!" said Kelly, taking a second nacho. "How'd you make these so good?"

"Exceptional talent?" Gayle suggested.

"Ewwww!" Rita held up her glass suspiciously. "This stuff's got little green bugs in it!"

"O, spare me thy ignorant prattle!" Gayle glared at Rita. "In yon pitcher did I concoct a toothsome mix of limeade, seltzer, lime juice, and"—she tapped Rita's glass—"grated lime peel."

"Oh, lime peel." Rita took a teeny sip. "Hey, it's good."

I tried mine. Gayle had made the limeade sweet and tart and tangy all at the same time. When it came to food, she was a natural. Could there be a way to make her cooking ability work for her Student Council campaign? Suddenly, a Great Idea began bubbling over in my brain.

"Gayle!" I said, ignoring all my mother's lecturing about talking with my mouth full. "Can you make this limeade in big batches?"

"I guess. Why?"

"Operation Limeade! It's a sure thing!" I headed for my mom's workroom and brought back five large sheets of stiff poster board.

"But we're supposed to make birth certificates next," complained Rita. "Plus design the covers for our egg-baby books."

"They can wait. I've got a Great Idea for Gayle's campaign." I surveyed the group. "You all *do* want to help Gayle win the election, don't you?"

Everyone nodded.

"Okay, we're going to make signs," I told them. "And they won't just say, 'Gayle for President.' They'll be more mysterious and say, 'This way to Gayle's limeade!' And each sign will have an arrow leading to the next sign and finally to the cafeteria, and there will be Gayle, ladling out her fabulous limeade and asking kids to vote for her!"

"Aren't there, like, rules against bringing food into the school?" asked Rita.

"Classes have bake sales," I reminded her.

"She better leave out that peel stuff, though. I swear, I thought it was bugs."

Gayle looked as if she was trying to make the connection between the limeade and the qualifications for Student Council president.

"You get along with Mrs. Hammer, right?" I asked her.

"Being a good eater helps one get along with the school cook," Gayle admitted.

"Then limeade can be just the first step. The whole week before the election, you can whip up delicious snacks for everybody and tell them that if you're elected you'll work with Mrs. Hammer to improve the quality of the school lunches!"

I smiled around at everyone. No one looked quite as happy as I felt, but they were nodding. I volunteered my mom to donate some cans of frozen limeade and my dad to let us have a box of little paper cups from his office. Kelly offered to bring in a few limes, and Sandra said we could count on her for seltzer.

I handed out the poster board and then selected a thick green marker from the cookie tin in the middle of the table. "Let's start with the signs leading to the cafeteria. Write 'This way to Gayle's limeade.' "

Sandra reached for a blue marker. As she picked it up, her elbow accidentally knocked against something resting near the table's edge. We all looked on in helpless horror as Natasha went crashing to the floor.

R.I.P.

Before school started on Thursday, I opened the library door and peeked in. Ms. Wong was behind the checkout desk, stamping a book for a third-grader. Sandra had begged Kelly and me to come with her to help her explain about Natasha. As the third-grader exited, we three went into the library.

Ms. Wong looked up and smiled when she saw us.

"Um, Dr. Wong?" Sandra began.

The smile faded from Ms. Wong's face. "Oh, dear. Do we have a patient for Library Hospital?"

Tears welled up in Sandra's eyes and her chin started to quiver. She shook her head.

"It's more like a victim for the Library Morgue," I said.

Slowly, Sandra lifted a wad of tissues toward Ms. Wong. Peeling back the top layers, she revealed what was left of Natasha. Her shell was smashed and had mostly fallen away, exposing large chunks of her white insides. Even her hard-boiled little yolk was cracked. "I knocked her off a table," Sandra confessed. "By accident."

Ms. Wong put an arm around her. "Just be glad your mom didn't drop you on your head," she said, trying to be cheerful.

Sandra wiped the back of her hand across her nose. "Do I flunk library?"

Ms. Wong shook her head.

"Do . . . do I get another egg-baby?"

Ms. Wong shook her head again. "I'm afraid not."

"Can Sandra and I both take care of my egg?" asked Kelly.

"Certainly," said Ms. Wong. "But if you make it to the end of the eggsperiment, you'll have to decide which one of you gets to participate in Mr. Sherman's activity."

At this, Sandra bit her lower lip. Natasha's shocked shell meant no Shell Shock!

"That's fine with me," Kelly said. "We can flip a coin at the end."

"No, that's okay." Sandra gave Kelly a grateful look. Then she glanced down at the mess in her hand. "What do I do with Natasha?"

"What would you like to do?" asked Ms. Wong. Sandra just stood there, holding her egg and sniffling. "I don't know," she cried as the 8:20 bell sounded in the hall.

"Come on," I said, pulling Sandra toward the library door. "We'll give Natasha a humdinger of a funeral!"

Sandra was still in bad shape when we got to our room, so Roger Rupp, the vice-chair, ran the class meeting. Kelly raised her hand and announced that a service for Natasha would be held at the 10:30 recess. I expected that a few kids might giggle and make fun of the idea of a funeral for a hard-boiled egg, but nobody did. Since Rita had spilled the beans about her little discovery in Mr. Sherman's desk drawer, everyone knew that Sandra had good reason to mourn.

At recess, we all gathered around the big oak in the side yard. Of course, we brought our eggs with us. Eddie carried his shoe box under one arm. Inside was Stan the Man, named for a former Cardinal baseball great. Barney held his carton open so his egg could witness the burial of the unfortunate Natasha. He was calling his egg Binky, after a parakeet of his that had long since died, and even though he hadn't spent much time penciling on Binky's face, he seemed genuinely fond of his egg-baby.

Ms. Wong came and Mr. Sherman did, too. He volunteered to hold Captain Kirk, Michael's egg, because Sandra had asked Michael to lead the service, and Michael thought maybe he wouldn't look dignified with a spaceship wobbling around on his head.

Michael cleared his throat. "Dearly beloved—"

"Michael!" Rita giggled. "That's what you say to start a wedding!"

Michael tried again. "Ladies and gentlemen, we are here this morning to say a few last words for Natasha, the recently departed egg of Sandra Guth."

In the silence that followed, Michael looked around at us. "So say a few words," he stage-whispered.

At last, Kelly said, "Natasha could do a fine somersault."

"Natasha had beautiful dark hair," chimed in Rita.

With that, Sandra started crying again.

"And beautiful, big brown eyes," Rita went on, "and beautiful lips and—"

"And we will all miss Natasha," Gayle interrupted firmly.

"We'll remember her when we see this," I said, holding up the big smooth rock that Barney had dug up somewhere for a tombstone. Kelly had painted on it:

NATASHA
EGG OF SANDRA
R.I.P.

"Why does it say *rip* on the tombstone?" Rita whispered to Kelly.

"It stands for Rest in Peace," Kelly whispered back. "There wasn't room to put it all on the rock."

Now Eddie bent down. He brushed aside some acorns and began scooping a hole in the dirt with a big spoon that Mrs. Hammer had lent us. Watching him, I thought about how unfair it all was. Here were the rest of us with our new egg-babies, thinking about how to make their birth certificates and writing in our egg-baby books, and there was Sandra without an egg-baby anymore. She'd never see Natasha again. I knew it was just an old hen's egg, but still, we were supposed to pretend they were our babies, weren't we? And something awful like this *could* happen to a real baby. Thinking about that gave me the same feeling I'd had when I thought about the boy who'd blown his fingers off with the cherry bomb. Awful things can happen—happen in a split second—and when they do, there's no way in the world to unhappen them.

Eddie stood up and Sandra knelt down, gently laying Natasha, tissues and all, inside the hole. Eddie scraped the dirt over the egg and smoothed the surface. When he finished, I put the stone on top.

Then we all just stood there, looking at our feet. Nobody knew what to do next. In about half a minute, Roger and Tim, who were in the back, sidestepped off in the direction of the lower field, and after that, a few at a time, everyone just walked away.

"It was a lovely service. Jennifer and Jonathan

NATASHA
EGG OF SANDOR
R.I.P

will never forget it," Rita told Sandra as we headed for the usual girls-against-boys soccer game. "And it's like a mega-tragedy that you'll miss out on Shell Shock!"

"Shut up, Rita!" Sandra snapped. Then she sped away from our group and down to the field, no doubt hoping that a good, hard game would help her forget her sorrows.

Gayle, Rita, and I were the last ones to reach the field. Michael and Sandra were kicking the ball around, warming up. The rest of the kids were standing on the sidelines, arguing.

"They'll be okay here," claimed Roger, pointing to his shoe box, which lay on the ground.

Tim set his box down next to Roger's.

"I don't know," said Kelly. "It's taking a chance."

Tim picked his box up again.

"Can't we just play?" begged Eddie.

"Let's move the boxes back from the field," Gayle suggested.

"But we have to keep them with us," objected Kelly.

"Leaving them here isn't exactly keeping them with us, is it?" asked Gayle. "Ten feet farther away and there's less chance of a stray ball hitting them."

The shoe boxes were positioned farther from the field, yet still within eye range. But I noticed that, even with all her brave words, Gayle put Albert's box in a protected position at the very back of the bunch.

"Well, *I'm* not leaving Jonathan and Jennifer all by themselves where they might get trampled to bits." Rita strutted off to some nearby swings, where she began pushing her basket back and forth, and making mushy little cooing sounds to her eggs.

The rest of us took our positions on the field. Gayle jogged over to the goalposts. Known behind her back, I am sorry to say, as the Roly-Poly Goalie, Gayle had a size advantage when it came to goal-tending. Wearing Bertha's pack, I took my customary position as fullback, where, it seemed to have been determined by the kids who were always the captains, I could do my team the least harm. For Sandra or Eddie, who really threw themselves into sports, playing soccer with an egg-baby on their backs might have been dangerous. But not much action ever came in my direction, and when it did, I usually got out of the way.

Eddie kicked off to Michael, who started dribbling toward the girls' goal, his spaceship sprong-ing around on top of his head like some kind of a crazy yo-yo. Halfway down the field, he tried to pass the ball to Tim, but Sandra intercepted and took off in the opposite direction, elbowing away any boys who came too close. On she charged to the boys' goal. Barney was a hard goalie to get around, but today, at the last second, as Sandra came in for the kill, he glanced over at the eggs. Bingo! It was one-nothing, girls' favor.

"Barney!" shouted Tim. "What'd you do that for?"

"Yeah!" yelled Jason. "Keep your eye on the ball!"

"You keep *your* eye on the ball!" Barney shouted back. "I quit!"

With that, Barney stomped off the field and snatched up his egg carton.

"Me, too!" declared Kelly, following Barney's lead. "It isn't worth maybe missing Shell Shock for some dumb soccer game!"

The captains repositioned the players they had left, and Eddie kicked off, but the game never really got going again. It just kind of limped along, with more than the usual number of out-of-bounds kicks, and lots more worried looks over at the eggs. Several other kids quit. Finally the only ones left, besides Eddie, either didn't have an egg anymore (Sandra) or had portable egg homes (Michael and me) or still hadn't gotten around to bringing in a shoe box (Jason).

As the bell rang to end morning recess, Eddie kicked hard at a clump of grass. "What a dorky game!" he shouted to no one in particular. "I hate these stupid eggs!"

GAYLE'S LIMEADE

"Oops! I promised to take that back to Mrs. Hammer," said Gayle, when we passed Natasha's grave and saw the spoon still lying under the tree. She tugged at my backpack. "Come with me."

"Careful of Bertha. We don't want to have another funeral." We ran up the lower-school steps. "Now we can ask Mrs. Hammer about serving the limeade tomorrow."

"Lila, are you sure the limeade's a good idea?"

"It's a Great Idea. Trust me."

We found Mrs. Hammer up to her elbows in soapsuds, scouring a lasagna tray. As she listened to our idea for the limeade, she nodded, causing the little green metallic disks on her hairnet to flicker under the bright cafeteria lights. "You'd just be giving out sample tastes, wouldn't you? I don't want anyone to skip drinking their milk."

"Just the tiniest little tastes," I assured her.

Mrs. Hammer said that Gayle could use her biggest stewpot for mixing the limeade, and, in return, we said we'd not only wash whatever utensils Gayle used but would also help her with tomorrow's pots and pans.

On Friday morning, I got a late start and didn't have time to put up our campaign posters before school. Mr. Sherman wouldn't let Gayle and me out of class, because he didn't want us to miss hearing the next chapter of *Great Expectations*. In this one, Pip is invited to visit this really weird old lady, Miss Havisham, who lives in a dark, cobwebby house. She's totally wrinkled and yellow and withered, but what's really creepy is that she's dressed in a moldy old bride's dress—the one she'd been wearing years and years ago when her groom jilted her on their wedding day!

As Mr. Sherman finished reading, he gave Gayle and me a nod. It was only ten minutes before lunch period began, so we had to move fast. Gayle zoomed down to the cafeteria to mix up her ingredients. I dropped to my hands and knees in the hallway and, as fast as I could, made tape rolls for the back of the first big THIS WAY TO GAYLE'S LIMEADE! poster.

I put Kelly's sign up by the stairs on the main floor. The lettering on her poster was by far the neatest, and I thought it should be seen first.

As I backed up to check whether the poster was straight, I stepped on someone's foot. Jumping off quickly, I lost my balance and ended up sitting on the floor.

"Sorry, Ms. Wong!" I exclaimed when I saw who it was bending over, rubbing her instep. "Are you okay?"

"I'm fine, Lila." Ms. Wong slipped her shoe back on and offered me a hand up.

On my feet again, I checked to make sure Bertha had survived my tumble. She had. Then I saw that Ms. Wong was looking at Kelly's poster.

"Gayle's running for president of Student Council," I explained. "She makes this great limeade and she's serving it today so the voters will get to know her."

Ms. Wong nodded. "And they will associate her with something delicious, is that it?"

"That's our strategy," I said. "I'm her campaign manager."

"Oh, so you like to manage things?"

"I guess. To tell you the truth, I was sort of hoping to run for president myself, but Gayle got nominated first, so I'm helping her."

"Well, good luck to you both," said Ms. Wong. She walked on down the hall and I got back to work putting tape rolls on Rita's poster, which I slapped up on the stairway wall. It had fancy curlicue lettering and a border made of limes that, when I backed away from the poster, now looked to me like a lot of green peas. Oh, well. I didn't have time to be picky. At the bottom of the stairs,

I put up my own poster. The bell for first lunch period rang as I was sticking the one Gayle had made on the wall right outside the cafeteria. The only big poster I had left was Sandra's. Hers simply read, GAYLE'S LIMEADE. I noticed that some of the letters had gotten squished together at the end, and then I remembered that Sandra had made this poster right after Natasha had taken her fall. No wonder it was a little messy! I quickly stuck it, along with two smaller VOTE FOR GAYLE! signs, high on the wall right behind the candidate.

I gave an O.K. sign to Mrs. Hammer, who was tending the fish sticks, wearing a hairnet dotted with sparkly plastic shells and sea horses. I turned to Gayle. "Ready?"

"I'm ready! Ready for love!" Gayle sang the Shell Shock lyric and boogied around the limeade table, jabbing the air with a soup ladle.

I whisked Albert's shoe box from the table so it wouldn't get knocked off, and then I stood back and waited to see my plan unfold.

I didn't have to wait long.

Mrs. Apple led her fifth-graders into the cafeteria in an orderly line. I could tell from the mystified looks on the kids' faces that they were wondering what the story was with the THIS WAY TO GAYLE'S LIMEADE! signs. When Mrs. Apple headed for the teachers' lounge, the line broke up.

"This way, folks!" Gayle beckoned the fifth-graders over to her table like a ringmaster at a circus. "Step right up for the taste treat of the decade!"

"Try some of Gayle's delicious limeade!" I called.

Zoe Rupp, Roger's frizzy-haired younger sister, was the first to come up to the table. "What's it cost?" she asked.

"It's free for one and all." Gayle handed her a cup. "Try some!"

Zoe took the little cup and raised it to her lips. But as she did so, Rob Boxer, a fifth-grade boy known for his big mouth, shoved his way to the table and yelled in Zoe's ear, "Don't do it!"

Startled, Zoe dropped the cup, splashing limeade all over Gayle's shirt.

"Look what it says!" shouted Rob, pointing to a spot above Gayle's head. Following Rob's finger, I saw only the GAYLE'S LIMEADE sign. Okay, so it wasn't the world's neatest poster. I didn't see what the big deal was.

Then all of a sudden everyone in Mrs. Apple's class started making choking, strangling sounds and sticking their fingers down their throats as if they were about to throw up.

"Hey!" I yelled over the noise. "What's the problem? It's delicious, really. Try some!" I picked up a cup that Gayle had already ladled out. "See?" With a flourish, I drank it down.

But this only made the fifth-graders cough and sputter all the more. They were yelling things like, "Gross-o-rama!" and "Slimeball!"

Ms. Rains led her fourth-grade class into the cafeteria then, and Rob called out, "Step right up, everybody! Try some of Gayle's slime!"

Slime? My head whirled around again, and now

I saw Sandra's poster the way Rob had seen it from the start:

"Yuck, slime-time!" It was the fourth-graders' turn to gag and stagger around holding their throats, while the poor cafeteria monitors tried to restore some order.

Slowly, Gayle turned to view the offending poster. "Gayle slime," she read under her breath, and then she whirled around to face me. "Lila Fenwick! I knew I shouldn't have listened to you! You and your stupid ideas! I quit!"

"You're letting this one little . . . goof . . . turn you into a quitter?"

"*One* little goof?"

I thought for a moment. "Okay, so the Girl Power thing didn't work out all that well either, but . . ."

Gayle held up her hand to silence me.

"But we can come up with something else," I went on quickly. "We've got time. The election's a whole week away. We'll think of something good! Something great!"

Just then Mrs. Hammer appeared with aprons

for us to wear as we started in on the baking pans. "You two can eat with the lower-school shift," she said.

Gayle narrowed her eyes at me. "I may have to go through with the election," she growled, "but the campaign's over, Lila. Trust me."

IMAGINE

On Saturday morning, I was sitting at the kitchen table, stirring my cereal into a soggy mess and wondering how I could get back into Gayle's good graces. She was mad. Not out-and-out furious, like the time I'd accidentally fixed it so she couldn't go trick-or-treating on Halloween, but a brooding, sulky kind of bad-mood mad—except when she was walking down the hall at school and someone called out, "Hey, Super Slime!" Then she'd smile a scary-looking smile and it looked as if any minute smoke would come pouring out of her ears.

My mom breezed into the kitchen. "I have to run over to the clinic for a couple hours," she said.

"Why don't you come with me? You've never even seen my office."

"Now you work on Saturdays, too?"

"Next week will be a lot easier if I can clear some paperwork off my desk today. Come with me. You can get a start on your homework, and when I'm finished, we can go out to lunch."

With Gayle mad at me, I had nothing better to do, so I grabbed my book bag, put Bertha in her pack, and we three drove into Clayton, parking in the lot behind the clinic. Inside, I followed my mom through a maze of exercise equipment to a tiny room at the end of the hall. "Here it is," she exclaimed, throwing open the door. "My very own office!"

The room was so small it seemed more like a closet. It had little windows, way up high, a wall of bookshelves, two chairs, and a cluttered desk. How could my mom prefer to be cooped up in here to being home? On her desk, practically hidden by a stack of papers, was a hinged silver picture frame. On one side was a photo of my dad holding a fly rod and a fat trout. On the other side, I recognized my squinty last year's school photo. But stuck into the frame on the outside of the glass was a snapshot.

"Hey, you can't even see my picture!" I leaned forward to find out who was important enough to cover up the top half of my head. It was a boy, an almost TKO boy, with wavy brown hair. He wore a T-shirt and cutoffs, but on one hand he also wore a dark glove.

"Oh, I'm sorry, Lila." My mom pulled the snapshot from the frame and thumbtacked it to her bulletin board.

"Is this the boy you were telling us about the other night? The one with the cherry bomb?"

My mom nodded.

"He gave you his picture?"

"I asked him for one, as a kind of Before."

"Does he always wear that glove?"

"For now." She gazed at his picture and sighed like somebody in love or something. "I'm hoping he'll take it off one of these days, and then he'll be able to try things with his right hand that he can't do as long as he keeps it on."

I tried to imagine what he must feel like. If he didn't wear the glove, other kids would stare at his mangled hand. Maybe he thought they'd avoid him so they wouldn't have to see it. I could sort of understand why he wanted to keep wearing the glove.

My mom cleared off a corner of her desk for me. I settled Bertha on the bookshelf where she couldn't topple off, and opened to Assignment 3 in Ms. Wong's booklet. IMAGINE, it said at the top.

Ah-ha! My specialty.

"Imagine what your new egg-baby is like. Present your findings to the class in an imaginative way."

I gazed up at Bertha. She stared back at me out of her big brown eyes. Magic Marker eyes. Thanks to a little circle of Velcro I'd glued to her side, she was holding her teddy bear, but still, it wasn't all that easy to imagine that Bertha was a real baby.

"Mom?"

"Hmmm?"

"What was I like when I was a week old?"

My mom looked up from her papers. "You were . . . needy. You needed to be fed every two or three hours and you needed your diapers changed about that often, too, and you needed to be bathed and burped and bounced. The only thing you didn't seem to need much was sleep."

"You don't make me sound like much fun!"

"Fun? Well, you weren't, exactly. I don't think any first-time parent is quite prepared for how utterly exhausting it is to have a new baby."

I scowled at my mother across the desk. I hadn't been fun. I'd been needy. She probably wished she had a handsome son, like old what's-his-name in the picture over there!

"But what a miracle you were," my mom went on, "with your deep blue eyes . . ."

"I've got green eyes," I snapped.

"They started out blue. Lots of babies' eyes change color. And your skin was so soft and you smelled heavenly. Have you ever smelled a brand-new baby?"

"Don't they just smell like diapers?"

"There's that, too, but a new baby's skin is the most delicately fragrant thing in the world."

"Did you love me?" I blurted out.

"Of course!" My mom laughed. "It's my theory that God makes babies absolutely adorable so that their parents can't help falling head over heels in love with them, and then they don't mind all the fussing and the diapers and waking up in the middle of the night for feedings."

"But the stuff you're saying is all about how hard it is!"

My mom looked confused. "Well, it *is* hard work taking care of an infant! But infancy doesn't last long. Babies grow up so fast and need their parents less and less. Before you know it, your helpless little baby has turned into an independent eleven-year-old."

I thought I could see my mom's eyes getting kind of wet around the bottom edges. "Tears will mess up your mascara!" I warned, which was a big joke, because she never wore any makeup.

"But I want you to understand that your father and I look back on your first few weeks as one of the best times in our lives. We loved you so much that every little thing you did seemed like a marvel. You had such funny expressions and you'd change them so fast—from sad to happy to puzzled, all in a couple of seconds." Shaking her head, she added, "If only you could have talked back then, I'll bet you could have told us some amazing things about how it felt to be a baby." She smiled at me, dry-eyed, thank goodness. "Have I answered your question?"

"Better than you know," I said, grabbing up my notebook and pencil just in time to give birth to a Great Idea for imagining baby Bertha.

First thing Monday morning, I found Gayle in line for the drinking fountain.

"Do me another favor?" I asked her.

"Surely you jest."

"It's for our egg reports. Please?"

Gayle stepped up for her turn at the fountain. She took a long drink and then straightened up, wiping her chin with her sleeve. I could tell she was just about to give in when a fourth-grader skidded into the line and yelled, "Outta my way, Slimehead!"

Gayle glowered at me and stomped off.

We were having a math test before recess, and I needed every free moment to cram for it, so I didn't even try to find anyone else to assist with my presentation on baby Bertha before Mr. Sherman dismissed us for library period. As we were choosing our books, I asked Lynn Williamson if she'd help me and she agreed. For what I had in mind, a ham like Gayle was just the ticket, but I had to make do with someone who was speaking to me, so I handed Lynn the page I'd written at my mom's office. "Your part starts here."

Lynn nodded and began giving it a quick read.

After we'd checked out our books, Ms. Wong had us sit in a circle again.

"Ms. Wong?" Eddie raised his hand. "Can't we take a break from the eggs at recess? It's no fun just sitting there, watching a bunch of old shoe boxes."

"Yeah," chimed in Tim. "Even tickets for the Shell Sh—"

"Tim!" Kelly cried.

Tim clapped a hand over his mouth. "Oops!"

Ms. Wong either didn't hear him or pretended she hadn't.

Eddie kept on. "There's no way we can play soccer!"

"Being responsible for someone else isn't easy," said Ms. Wong.

"I had to go to my art class last night," volunteered Kelly, "and I asked my grandfather to baby-sit for my egg. He said he would, but I could tell he thought it was really stupid, baby-sitting an egg with a drawn-on face."

"Did you explain the eggsperiment to him?" asked Ms. Wong.

"Kind of, but he just shook his head and asked me if they still taught reading and arithmetic at school."

Ms. Wong gave a wilted smile. Her Great Eggspectations were meeting with some opposition.

"Do we have to do this much longer?" asked Tim.

"Through next week," said Ms. Wong briskly. "Now, who would like to present what they have imagined about their egg-babies?"

Rita's hand popped up first.

"I imagine Jonathan," she read, "as a perfect baby. He never cries and is always smiling. He loves to be dressed up in his little sailor suit and to go out in his stroller."

Rita turned the page in her egg-baby book.

"Jennifer is just as perfect as Jonathan," she read. "She coos and gurgles in her playpen for hours."

Rita went on and on, telling about how Jonathan and Jennifer liked to go to birthday parties and ride little ponies, until finally Ms. Wong had to stop her to let someone else have a turn.

Oddly enough, Barney had his hand up and was ooh-ooh-oohing to be called on.

"Binky is a good egg," he read, looking up and chuckling at his own joke. "He licks it . . ." Barney scowled at his handwriting. "He *likes* it when I jounce him up and down on my knee and make up funny songs for him." He took his egg out of the carton and held it on his knee.

> Little baby Binky-boo
> Bounces like a kangaroo!

He grinned over at Ms. Wong. "That's all."

"Thank you, Barney. Did you by any chance ask your mother or father about what you used to like when you were a baby?"

"Yeah. My dad told me he used to do that to me, but he'd say Barney-boo." He made a silly face. "That's not cheating, is it?"

"Quite the opposite," said Ms. Wong. "Good parenting skills are passed along in just that way." She looked around the room. "Okay, who wants to go next? Lila?"

"Lynn's going to help me present mine."

My co-star stood up, holding the script I'd given her. I unzipped my purple backpack and propped it on my chair, with Bertha sitting up in plain view. Then I crouched down behind the chair. Lynn started reading. I'd expected her voice to be barely above a whisper, but to my surprise she read her part with lots of expression.

LYNN: *Greetings! I'm Tanya Talkshow of "Look Who's Here!" on WBABY-TV, and today I'm interviewing Baby Bertha van Egg. Just how old are you, Bertha?*

ME: *About a week . . . whatever that is.*

LYNN: *So tell me, Bertha, what's it like to be one week old?*

ME: *It's pretty frustrating, actually. I can't do anything for myself . . . except cry. When I'm hungry, I cry. When I need a nap, I cry. When I mess up my diaper, I cry. When I need to burp, I cry. I just hope that my mom can figure out which cry means what.*

LYNN: *Hmmm, I don't want to hurt your feelings, Bertha, but it sounds like you're kind of a crybaby.*

ME: *Well, I bet you were, too, when you were my age!*

LYNN: *Take it easy, Bertha! So, what are your plans for the future?*

ME: *Well, Tanya, I'm thinking about growing a little hair sometime soon and maybe pushing up a few teeth. But mainly I just plan to hang out with my mom and suck on my toes and things.*

LYNN: *Sounds exciting! Thank you for being our guest today on "Look Who's Here!" I'm Tanya Talkshow saying ta-ta!*

I'd been hoping that this little interview would be worthy of applause, and evidently it was. Lynn and I took a few bows. No one else volunteered to present what they'd imagined about their babies, so Ms. Wong offered to give her baby-sitter's quiz to anyone who felt ready to take it, but no one volunteered for that, either. After saying that our last three assignments would be due next Monday, Ms. Wong dismissed us to recess a few minutes early. As we left, I thought she looked kind of tired.

Spacehead Michael and the eggless kids talked their way into the fifth-grade soccer game. For some reason Gayle walked over to watch. Everybody else sprawled out under the big oak tree, near where Natasha and a few of her buddies were buried. Sitting down beside Kelly, I surveyed the egg cemetery and thought about how each of its occupants had met its untimely end.

HENRIETTA EGG
R.I.P.

Harriet Horner's older sister said she'd sit for Henrietta, but then she got asked out on a date and was too embarrassed to take along a shoe box, so she put the egg in her pocketbook, where it got squished, and then she had the nerve to tell Harriet that she owed her a new purse!

EVA EGG
R.I.P.

Barb Fox accidentally sat on Eva.

HARRY EGG
R.I.P.

ELSA EGG
R.I.P.

TYRANNOSAURUS EGG
R.I.P.

These three little rocks didn't have actual egg-bodies underneath them. Maury Weinstock's German shepherd had eaten Harry Egg. Roger Rupp's little brother, Frankie, had caused Tyrannosaurus Egg to become extinct by bashing it with a little toy hammer and then smooshing the results all over Roger's science book. And Maisie McDowell's mother, who insisted that Elsa Egg be put in the refrigerator each night to keep it from spoiling, had mistakenly used Elsa to make Maisie an egg-salad sandwich one morning, when her eyes were half shut because she hadn't had her coffee yet. Maisie detected the horrible mistake when she went to get Elsa to take her to school, and of course she hadn't *eaten* the sandwich, but Barney was calling her Cannibal anyway.

Kelly and Lynn were finishing up yet another silly hand-clapping game. With egg-babies to take care of, that was about all it was safe to play. Soccer was impossible. Not that I minded all that much, since soccer wasn't exactly my forte, but I hated to see my friends so down in the dumps. Nothing seemed worth everybody being in a funk all the time, not even the promise of seeing Shell Shock.

As I sat there thinking, a truly electric Great Idea for ending the recess blues shocked me into action. I jumped up.

"Where are you going?" asked Kelly.

"Back to the library," I called over my shoulder. "There's something I want to check out!"

CODDLED EGGS

Tuesday morning before school, I took the baby-sitter's quiz. I had to answer questions on what information I'd ask a baby's parents to give me before they went out and on what I'd do in case of different emergencies. After she'd graded it, Ms. Wong said that if she had a child, she'd feel perfectly comfortable leaving me in charge. She gave me a little button with a picture of a crawling baby on it to show that I'd passed.

I made it to class just in time to hear Sandra pounding on Mr. Sherman's desk with her language-arts book and shouting, "Will the meeting please come to order, guys!"

When Sandra called for Old Business, Michael

reminded everyone that the Student Council assembly, where each candidate would give a three-minute speech, would be this Friday.

Under New Business, Barney announced that he'd actually done his math homework, but then he'd lost it, and if anyone found it, to let him know. When no one else had any New Business, I raised my hand. I'd saved the best for last.

"This morning at recess," I said, standing beside my desk, "the Coddled Egg Day-Care Center will be open for business."

Everyone looked at me like maybe I'd lost my marbles.

"I passed Ms. Wong's test, see?" I pointed to my baby button. "So now I'm qualified to sit for other people's eggs."

"Whoopee!" shouted Eddie. "Back to soccer!"

"Pipe down," ordered Sandra.

"It's a great deal," I added. "I'm only charging a quarter per egg per recess."

"Is there a discount for twins?" asked Rita.

"I'll think about it," I said. "And since probably no one has any extra money with them today, I'm accepting IOU's. You can pay me tomorrow."

"All right, Lila!" called out Barney.

I sat down, feeling happier than I'd been since the first day of school when I'd been full of hope for this sixth-grade year and my part in it. Coddled Eggs, I felt sure, was one of my Greatest Ideas yet.

The classroom clock finally made it to 10:30, time for morning recess. I stationed myself on the shady side of the big oak, slightly away from the egg graveyard. Within five minutes, about half the kids in my class had given me little scraps of paper saying, "IOU 25¢."

I positioned eleven shoe boxes, one cigar box, and one egg carton close to the tree trunk and sat down next to them. Thirteen little babies, whose mothers and fathers had gone off to work. "I know just how you feel," I told them.

Leaning back against the tree, I closed my eyes. A gentle breeze tickled my face. Birds twittered and squirrels chattered above my head. Ah, this was the life. Not only would I avoid humiliating myself by tripping over my own feet in soccer, but I was also making money just by sitting here. The world seemed peaceful and full of possibilities.

Figures danced in my head. Twenty-five cents times thirteen egg-babies equals . . . $3.25! I'd probably make $3.25 at afternoon recess, too. Maybe more. That was $6.50 a day! And this was only Tuesday. There were three more days this week, plus five days next week, which would make it eight days times $6.50. Even without math-whiz Gayle's help, I managed to figure out that by next Friday I'd have earned $58.50!

Whoa! That was more than enough to finish paying my parents back for my bike loan so I could start getting my allowance again, and I'd still have money left. Maybe I'd get the new Shell Shock album, *Big End Up*. Plus, there were always tons of things to buy at the Fall Festival booths.

If my mother had known what was going on inside my brain, she'd have said, "Lila, you're counting your chickens before they hatch." But I couldn't help myself. And besides, these chickens were never going to hatch!

As I sat there dreaming, a voice sounded close to my ear. "Are you athleep?"

Opening my eyes, I found myself face-to-face with Eddie's little cousin, Gloria. Two of her first-grade friends stood behind her.

"No," I said huffily.

"What are all these boxes?" asked the girl with brown pigtails whose name was Sara.

I reached over for the shoe box closest to me and opened it up. "See the egg?"

"Ooh, look, Tishie!" exclaimed Sara to a freckly girl who stood next to her. "It has a little face!"

"Right. This is Stan the Man, Eddie's egg."

"Eddie'th my couthin," said Gloria.

"I know," I told her. "See, all of us sixth-graders have an egg-baby to take care of, and—"

"Why?" interrupted Gloria.

"To learn how hard it is to be responsible for a baby."

"Even a egg-baby?" Tishie asked.

"Yes," I told her. "And it is hard because you have to keep your egg-baby with you all the time."

"Then why is everybody's eggs here?" asked Tishie.

"Because I passed a test on how to baby-sit, so I'm taking care of all the eggs while the other kids play soccer."

"We will help you," said Gloria.

"Oh, no, that's okay. I can handle it."

Gloria plopped down close to the shoe boxes. "We can take care of egg-babieth, too," she proclaimed, reaching for a shoe box, "jutht ath good ath thixth-graderth."

Tishie and Sara sat down on either side of her and each one grabbed a shoe box.

"Hands off the boxes!" I warned them. "If one of these eggs gets broken, I will be in major trouble."

"Thith one ithn't shut up in a bokth," Gloria said.

I closed the top of Binky's egg carton. "It is now."

"But we want to see the babies," whined Tishie.

"Okay, okay, I'll show them to you, but you are not to put so much as a finger on any of these boxes. Promise?"

They promised, but just to be on the safe side, I made them hold their hands behind their backs, too. Then I opened each lid and showed them the egg-baby inside, carefully closing the box when they were finished looking, and putting it in a safe place.

"That's all the babies," I told them at last. "Go play now."

"No," insisted Gloria. "We will thtay and help you."

"Come on," said Tishie. "We can play Horse Needle."

"I'm the vet!" shouted Sara.

Tishie and Gloria scrambled to their feet and galloped away, neighing and whinnying at the top of their lungs. Sara tore off after them, shouting, "Come, Socksie! Come, Brownie! You got to get your shots!"

When they'd gone, I checked all the egg-babies to make sure they'd survived the first-grade snoopers. Then I lined the boxes up in their original places, opening Binky's egg carton just the way Barney had done. Everything seemed under control until a red rubber ball came bouncing to the tree. I ran and scooped it up before it got close to the eggs. "Play your game farther away!" I called to the two first-grade boys running toward me, and then I heaved the ball to them. Turning around, I saw Gloria and Sara galloping around the tree. "You, too!" I shouted. "Play someplace else!"

"Lila!" I turned at the sound of my name and saw Ms. Wong on the sidewalk. She looked annoyed as she started walking toward me. "What's going on here? You passed your quiz and now you're sitting for"—she made a quick count of the boxes—"*thirteen* egg-babies?"

"Um, I've opened a day-care center."

Ms. Wong groaned. "You're not taking care of everyone's eggs all the time, are you?"

"Just at recess," I said sheepishly. "Is that wrong?"

"Well, no, not wrong exactly." Ms. Wong started

telling me all about how the eggsperiment was designed to teach responsibility, when, out of the corner of my eye, I spotted that ball again. "Excuse me," I muttered, running after the ball once more. This time, I kicked it to the far corner of the playground, and then came panting back to the tree. When I got there, Ms. Wong shook her head and laughed. "Looks as if you're becoming responsible the hard way!" she said. "Actually, this makes a lot of sense."

I figured I might as well make a full confession. "I'm charging a quarter per egg. Is that okay?"

Ms. Wong brightened. "Yes, that's fine. At least your friends will learn that turning responsibility over to someone else can be expensive."

The bell sounded to end recess. Ms. Wong walked off, and I turned back to where the egg homes were lined up under the tree. For a few minutes, everything was chaotic as all the kids came running up to me, happy and sweaty after their game. They scooped up their boxes and headed for the classroom. Within a minute, not a box was left.

But Barney still stood beneath the tree. He held out an empty egg carton in my direction. "Where's Binky?"

What could have happened? I'd checked the eggs after the little girls had left. "Maybe somebody took him inside."

Barney stabbed a finger at me. "You better find him!"

"Hey, don't worry!" Smiling broadly to hide the bad feeling that was fast coming over me, I looked all around the tree to make sure Binky hadn't rolled out of his carton and gotten lost among the egg gravestones. I didn't see him.

"Let's go back to the room," I suggested. "Someone must have picked him up for you."

I ran up the steps, Barney close at my heels. At our classroom door he roared out, "Okay, who took Binky?"

No one stepped forward with his egg.

Mr. Sherman walked in the door behind Barney. "Please take your seats, class, and get out your math folders."

Barney tugged on his shirtsleeve. "But, Mr. Sherman!" He held out his egg carton. "Binky's been kidnapped!"

Poor Barney was starting to cry. And what made me feel really terrible was that I knew he wasn't crying about the loss of a Shell Shock ticket. His family owned several movie theaters in town and had lots of connections. He could always get tickets to anything he wanted. Barney was crying over Binky.

"Don't worry, Barney!" I gave him a pat on the back. "I'll find Binky for you. I promise!"

He jerked away from my touch. "You better! You just better!"

I trudged over to my desk and got out my math folder. The whole time, I could hear Barney sniffling and shuffling a mess of papers around inside his desk. Mr. Sherman was up at the board drawing a flattened-out circle, which he said was an ellipse, but my mind was still on Binky. How could he have simply disappeared?

"Hey!" Barney yelled from behind his open desk. "I found a ransom note!"

Mr. Sherman stopped the lesson. "Mr. Barker, can this wait until . . ."

Barney slammed down his desk top and waved a piece of paper in the air. Then he started reading it out loud. "If you have $75.60 and Melissa has $42 . . ." He looked up from the paper. "Okay, who's Melissa?"

"Barney!" groaned Gayle. "That's an old math sheet. We had it for homework last week!"

Barney frowned down at the paper and then stuffed it back in his desk. "I thought it was kind of a high ransom."

Mr. Sherman sighed and turned back to his ellipse. But all I could see up on that board was a big, fat Binky Barker.

FENWICK'S WAY

At afternoon recess, Barney organized a boycott of Coddled Egg. Instead of playing soccer, everybody searched the playground and the lower field for Binky. After recess, I even looked for him inside Chocolate's guinea-pig cage, but none of us found so much as a clue.

By lunchtime the next day, Barney was threatening to adopt Bertha to take Binky's place. I was desperate. I needed Gayle and found her sitting by herself in the cafeteria, eating and reading. I put my lunch tray down across from hers. "Gayle, you have to help me."

"Mmmm." Gayle's eyes were glued to the page of her book.

"This is a crisis. Help me and my carrot cake is yours."

"One more chapter," Gayle mumbled.

I had just about decided that I was hungry enough to take a bite of what the cafeteria menu called Chicken à la King, when Gayle slammed her book. "Ah-ha!" she crowed. "I knew the dentist did it!"

"Did what?"

"Hid the microchip in the ballet dancer's filling."

"What are you reading?"

"*Sanchez's Way.*" Gayle reached over to my tray with her fork and harpooned my dessert. Our feud, it seemed, was over. "See, this private eye, Sanchez, hypnotizes witnesses and has them experience seeing a crime all over again in their heads. Then he asks them questions, and from what they tell him, he puts together his case." She took a big bite of my cake. "It's brilliant."

"Does that work? Can people really remember things like that when they're hypnotized?"

"Really. They can see everything just the way they did the first time, but they might be able to notice details that their conscious mind had forgotten."

As I watched the rest of my carrot cake disappear, a Great Idea appeared inside my head. "Gayle, that's what we can do!"

"*We?*" Gayle sprang halfway out of her chair. "Oh, no. I recognize that look. *We* are not doing anything!"

I reached across the table and grabbed her sweat-shirt. "Does that book give all the words Sanchez says when he hypnotizes people?"

"Yes, but . . ."

I pulled Gayle closer. "You think you could do it? Hypnotize someone, the way Sanchez does?"

She sat back down. "Maybe."

"Gayle, you have to hypnotize me. You have to tell me to remember what happened yesterday morning at recess, when everybody came to get their eggs. Maybe in my mind I'll be able to see who picked up Binky!"

"I don't know . . ."

I lowered my voice. "I think I already know who did it, but I've got to be sure."

"Who?"

"If I tell you, will you help me?"

"Oh, all right."

"That creep who calls me Toothpick Legs," I whispered.

"Tim?"

I nodded. "This morning before school, I saw him and Roger playing catch in the side yard, and Tim went running back to catch a high one and stomped right on his shoe box."

"Goodbye, baby."

"Right. When he opened up the box, I saw his egg and it was a total mess. It had one of those stupid dinosaurs sticking into it, and Roger said, 'Hey, it was a dinosaur egg!' and Tim just said, '*Was* is right.' "

"He wasn't upset?"

"Not a bit. He just tossed his shoe box, egg and all, into the trash."

"I still don't see how this incriminates him for kidnapping Binky."

"Listen to this. As they're walking into school, Roger says, 'There goes your Shell Shock ticket,' but Tim just shrugs and says, 'Who cares? There are other ways to get a ticket to that concert.'"

"But," Gayle objected, "how would Tim explain that suddenly his egg looked exactly like Barney's?"

"They both had beige eggs, like mine, and did you happen to notice what Barney used to draw Binky's face?"

Gayle shook her head.

"Pencil. Tim could just erase Binky's face and draw on another one."

Gayle started flipping through her book. "I'll read over the scene where Sanchez first hypnotizes the dental hygienist, and I'll try to hypnotize you the same way."

As Gayle was rereading her material, Rita came over, all smiles. "Guess what, Lila?" She tapped a pink-polished fingernail on a crawling-baby button pinned to her collar. "I passed the baby-sitting test, too."

"Congratulations."

"I'm starting a day-care center at afternoon recess."

"How original."

"And I'm only charging a dime. Mine's called Humpty Dumpty's Baby Basket."

"Humpty Dumpty? Wasn't he the egg that had a great fall?"

Rita wrinkled her nose at me.

"And an even worse winter? And a horrible spring?"

"For your information, Lila Fenwick, *Humpty Dumpty* is a nursery rhyme, and babies love nursery rhymes."

As Rita was blathering on, Barney shambled over to our table. "How come you're not out looking for Binky?"

"Don't worry, Barney, I'm about to look for him." I pointed to my head. "In here."

"Oh, right," scoffed Rita. "I'm sure Barney's egg is really lost somewhere inside your brain!"

"Huh?" said Barney.

"Gayle's going to hypnotize me," I informed them, "and then I'm going to relive the moment when everybody came to pick up their eggs yesterday. Gayle says I might be able to see something that I didn't notice when it happened."

"Like who stole Binky?"

"Eggsactly!"

Barney nodded as if he half understood. "But if this doesn't work, you have to hand over Bertha."

"It'll work, it'll work," I assured him, wondering what I'd do if it didn't.

"You gonna do it now?" asked Barney.

Gayle looked up from her book. "There isn't time now. We'll do it at afternoon recess."

When we went back to class, I kept an eye on Tim. True, I hadn't exactly seen him with a substitute egg, but my theory made sense. And, during language arts, Mr. Sherman called on Tim to give an example of a possessive pronoun and use it in a sentence.

"*My*," said Tim. "It is *my* egg now."

I rest my case.

By recess time, word of Gayle's enterprise had spread. Rita tried to drum up business for Humpty Dumpty's Baby Basket, but everyone was more interested in seeing if Gayle could really hypnotize me than in playing soccer.

Gayle was back to her old happy self: she had an audience and was ready to roll. "Let's do it"— she paused dramatically on the sidewalk—"under the tree where the crime occurred."

We all gathered beneath the oak.

"Lie down," Gayle commanded in a low, Sanchez-style voice.

I flipped off my Bertha pack, tucked it protectively under one arm, and lay down right in the spot where I'd been sitting so comfortably the morning before. Now the ground felt lumpy and an acorn stabbed into the back of my neck.

Gayle sat down by my head. "Close your eyes and relaaaaax." Her voice sounded like a tape being played at too slow a speed. "Take a deep breath in through your nooooose and let it out through your mooooooouth."

With everyone watching me, even breathing wasn't all that easy.

"Imagine," said Gayle, "that you are standing at the top of an escalator—"

"Like the one in the mall?"

"Silence!"

Without even opening my eyes, I could see the look that Gayle had to be giving Rita.

"Now, take in a breath and let it out slooooowly. Every time you let your breath out, you will feel more relaaaaaxed."

I took some deep breaths.

"Imagine that you are stepping onto the escalator. It is going down, and as it goes down, you feel more and more relaxed. It is going down, down, down."

I was on that escalator.

"Let your breath out even more slowly, now one more. The escalator is almost all the way down. When you step off, you will be in a peaceful place, totally relaxed, and you will be hypnotized. Step off now."

Inside my head, I stepped off. But I wondered if I was hypnotized. I didn't feel any different.

"You have entered a hypnotic state," declared Gayle. "This simply means that you are more relaxed than usual and will respond to my questions. Are you ready to begin?"

"Yessss."

"Picture in your mind yesterday's morning recess. You are sitting here, under the tree, with all the egg boxes."

"Yessss." Even though I was trying to make my "yeses" sound a little more theatrical than usual, I found myself picturing what Gayle was saying quite vividly.

Gayle's voice droned on. She described the bell ringing to end recess. I heard it loud and clear, and then I saw once more everybody streaming toward me. In the rush, I looked for Tim, but couldn't find him. Everyone scooped up a box. I kept my mind's eye on the egg carton, but saw it just sitting there, empty, until Barney picked it up.

"Did you see it, Lila?" Gayle asked me. "Did you see who took Binky?"

"Nooo."

"Hmmm. Did you see Barney's egg carton?"

"Yesss."

"Was Binky in it?"

"Nooo."

Gayle was quiet for a minute. "Okay, let's go back a bit. Picture the beginning of recess when Barney's bringing you his egg."

Instantly, I saw the scene that Gayle described; saw Barney kneeling down, putting his carton under the tree, saw him opening the lid, the way he'd done at Natasha's funeral, so that Binky wouldn't be in the dark. Then I saw him scrawling out my IOU.

"Can you see Barney's egg?"

"Yessss."

"Excellent. Keep watching that egg."

But as I watched, a familiar voice invaded my hypnotic state.

"What'th going on?"

"Lila's getting hypnotized," Eddie's voice answered. "Now beat it, Gloria."

"No," said Gloria. "Why ith Lila getting hypmatithed?"

"It has to do with our eggs," said Eddie. "Now go!"

"What about our eggth?"

"She's trying to figure out," Eddie said between clenched teeth, "who took Barney's egg."

"Oh," said Gloria. "Bye!"

As I heard the patter of her running feet, I sat up. "Gloria!" I shouted. "Come back here!"

"Lila!" Gayle jumped up and put her hands on her hips. "You can't snap out of a hypnotic trance that way! I have to bring you out of it, slowly."

"Like she has to ride up the escalator again?" asked Rita.

"She's supposed to." Gayle folded her arms across her chest. "Sanchez's subjects always do."

"If you get unhypnotized too fast, can't you get, like, brain damage?"

"Take a break, Rita!" I said, keeping my eye on the little girl slowly plodding back to where I was sitting. "Gloria, did you take Barney's egg?"

"I don't know."

I narrowed my eyes. "Did you take any egg?"

"You only thaid not to touch any egg *bokth*," sputtered Gloria, "and thith egg wathn't in a bokth."

"When did you do it?" I demanded.

"When you were talking to Mith Wong, but I only borrowed him!"

"Why?"

"Tho Mith Houghton could thee him," said Gloria. "Then the firtht grade could get egg-babieth, too."

"Then why didn't you bring him right back?"

Gloria shrugged. "I forgot."

Barney elbowed his way over to Gloria. "Where's Binky?"

"He'th in my dethk, but . . . ."

Barney grabbed her arm and hustled her off toward her classroom.

The case of the mysterious disappearance of Binky Barker had been solved. Gloria had filched him right out from under my nose. Who would ever trust me with an egg-baby again?

Goodbye, Coddled Egg.

Goodbye, $58.50.

Goodbye to one of my greatest Great Ideas ever.

WALLOW

Mr. Sherman read aloud to us every day for at least half an hour. But on Thursday he read one page, sighed, and shut *Great Expectations*. "I remember loving this book," he said, "and it is a great book, but I'm not sure it's the best book to read aloud to a sixth-grade class."

"Yeah," Barney agreed. "The only good part was in the beginning, when that guy escaped from jail."

"Am I right?" Mr. Sherman asked. "How many of you are really interested in what happens to Pip?"

Only Michael and Gayle raised their hands.

When I thought about weird old Miss Havisham,

I wanted to raise my hand, too, but the story of Pip was leaving me behind. Talk about a whiner! Here he was, this nobody of an apprentice blacksmith, dreaming all the time about becoming a rich gentleman, and when his dream mysteriously comes true, what does he do? He feels sorry for himself!

Whenever I feel sorry for myself, my mom tells me that she thinks I must enjoy "wallowing in self-pity." Hearing the word "wallow," even when I'm not hypnotized, brings to mind a clear picture of fat old pigs rolling around in sloshy, oozy mud, and loving it.

Mr. Sherman promised to begin reading us a more appropriate story the next day and said that he hoped when we were older we'd all give *Great Expectations* another try. He slid it between the bookends on his desk.

Goodbye, *Great Expectations*, I thought, but I felt as if I'd already said goodbye to my great expectations a couple of weeks ago. My high hopes for sixth grade had all fizzled. There'd be no Student Council office for me, and now I didn't even have Gayle's campaign to manage. I'd lost Barney's egg, destroyed everyone's confidence in Coddled Egg Day-Care, and turned Humpty Dumpty's Baby Basket into a thriving business. Plus, I still wondered what Tim had meant when he told Roger that there were other ways to get in to see the Shell Shock concert, so I asked him. After he finished accusing me of being a toothpick-leg spy, he just said he was planning to ask Barney if he could get him a ticket. Even my own mother seemed to care only about her patients these days, and she stuck me with all the chores at home. I felt that I had nothing to look forward to but a dreary life of homework and housework, language arts and laundry . . .

"Ms. Fenwick?"

I looked up from my mudhole. Mr. Sherman had obviously just asked me a question, but what it was, I had no idea.

"Yes, sir?"

"I've asked everyone please to get out a sheet of paper and write a paragraph about what features might be included in a school newspaper."

Great Ideas for a school paper, I wrote at the top of my page, and then I tried to concentrate. What should a paper have? I started a list.

   1. Cartoons
   2. Interviews with important kids

Like Gayle and Eddie, I thought, one of whom would soon be elected Student Council president. Or Kelly, who'd just won a painting competition at the mall, or Michael, who'd already started on his Science Fair project and was considered a contender for the big state prize this year.

And then another idea struck me.

   3. Interviews with not-so-important kids

This I could picture clearly.

REPORTER: *Hi, what's your name?*
ME: *Lila Fenwick.*
REPORTER: *Are you new here at Price School?*
ME: *No, I've been here since kindergarten.*
REPORTER: *Oh, so, what's your claim to fame?*
ME: *Well, I was lunch-line monitor once in second grade.*
REPORTER: *And what's the most important thing you've done in sixth grade?*
ME: *Uh, kept my desk neat, I guess.*
REPORTER: *Hmmmm. Do you have any exciting plans for the future?*
ME: *Next week, I'm going to arrange all my markers in alphabetical order by color and then . . .*

"Ms. Fenwick?"
Mr. Sherman towered over me again.
"Have you finished your paragraph?"
I looked down and was almost surprised to see that I'd actually written out my stupid imaginary interview. I started to crumple up my paper, but Mr. Sherman put his hand on top of it.
"But, Mr. Sherman, this isn't . . ."
"I'm sure it's very interesting." He added my paper to the others he had collected.
Oh, great! After he read what I'd written, Mr. Sherman would probably call my parents and recommend that I see the school psychologist. I tried

to concentrate on my book during free reading period, but just stared at one page until the 3:30 bell sounded. Then I walked straight to Mr. Sherman's desk.

"Please, can I have that paper back, Mr. Sherman?"

"Are you able?" he asked.

"I mean *may* I have it back? Please? It isn't exactly a paragraph about what should be in the school newspaper."

"No?"

"No, it was just sort of nothing, but I'll write a paragraph tonight, a really good one, if you'll just let me have this one."

"You must have been concentrating so hard during silent reading that you didn't see Ms. Wong come in and get the papers."

"You mean she has them?"

Mr. Sherman nodded.

Groaning, I grabbed my Bertha pack and my book bag and ran out of our classroom toward the library. But by the time I got there the lights were off and the door was locked.

The art teacher, Ms. Sherry, came down the hall and saw me standing there, hopelessly twisting the doorknob.

"Ms. Wong just left," she said. "Not two minutes ago."

"Thanks!" I started off for the parking lot. Maybe if I really sprinted, I could get there in time! But as I ran out the front door, I saw Ms. Wong at the wheel of her little red car, chugging past the school.

I sat down hard on the steps, catching my breath. The yard was practically empty now, but over by the flagpole I spotted Gayle and Michael. They were just standing there, talking. Michael was nodding so hard at something Gayle was saying that his spaceship wobbled dangerously on top of his head.

Relief flooded over me. At that moment, I couldn't think of anything better than telling my two best friends how miserable I felt.

"Hey!" I called, walking over to them.

They turned toward me, and to tell the truth, they both looked a little odd.

"Oh, hi, Lila." Gayle's voice sounded higher than usual. She shifted Albert E.'s shoe box to her other arm. I thought maybe she hadn't completely forgiven me for snapping out of my hypnotic trance too soon.

"Hi, Lila," said Michael.

Lila? Michael had never called me Lila in his life. What was going on?

"You guys walking home?" I asked.

They looked at each other and shrugged. For some reason, Gayle's face started turning red.

"You won't believe what I just did," I said as the three of us headed down the sidewalk. "You know that paragraph we were supposed to write? The one about the school paper?"

They nodded.

"Well, I was feeling kind of lousy and I started thinking, what if a reporter were interviewing me for the paper and . . ."

Suddenly it seemed like the hardest thing in the world to explain to Gayle and Michael how I'd felt and what I'd written.

"Anyway," I hurried on, "I wrote this strange interview instead of a paragraph and Ms. Wong'll probably think I'm nuts."

I'd hoped Gayle would say something about how if I wrote it, it was probably brilliant, but she only nodded and said, "Sounds weird."

We walked on in silence then, and not the usual comfortable silence, either. I thought maybe the cloud of my bad mood had expanded and settled over all of us.

At the turnoff to my house, I said, "See you, Michael."

"Later, Fenwick."

Then I noticed that Gayle wasn't turning with me.

"Aren't you coming over, Gayle?"

"Um, I don't think so," she said. "We hadn't really said anything about it, had we?"

"But you come over every day."

"Well, we've got this heavy-duty math home-work tonight and . . ."

I frowned. "I don't remember any big math assignment."

"It's just in the red book," said Michael.

The red book. That was Michael's nice way of

saying the advanced group. My math book was pea green.

"So," I said, "you're studying for it . . . together."

Gayle smiled uncomfortably.

And then it hit me like a ton of puky green math books—Gayle and Michael wanted to be alone! Just the two of them, without me!

"Oh, that's great! Well, good luck!" I babbled because I couldn't think what to say. I made my legs start walking toward my house. "If you run into any problems you can't solve, call me up. Haha!"

"See you, Lila!" Gayle called.

I broke into a run. Math, smath. They couldn't fool me. I knew what was going on! I knew why they wanted to be alone! I could just hear my once best friend! *Dost thou not wish to place a kiss upon this fair maiden's lips?* And then—smack smackeroo!

At last I reached our mailbox and leaned on it, panting for breath. How could I be so stupid? How could I not have seen right away that my two best friends liked each other, and were leaving me out in the cold?

Moping up the walk, I let myself into the too quiet house. I beelined for the refrigerator, hoping that a snack would cheer me up, but the state of the kitchen took my appetite away. In the sink were cereal bowls half filled with water. Fat, waterlogged Cheerios floated beside eggshells. Glasses covered with orange-juice pulp stood next to them. An egg-encrusted skillet topped the pile. Turning away from the mess, I spied yet another note from my mom:

> *Dear Lila,*
>
> *I know—it's a mess! I had to see a patient at 8:30 this morning and didn't have time to clean up. Think you could pitch in? Thanks for your help, honey!*
>
> *xoxo*
> *Mom*

Pitch in. That meant touching those gross Cheerios. After the day I'd had, I just couldn't face those dishes. Not right then. I needed to do something to make myself feel better, not worse. And all of a sudden I knew just what that something was.

Strapping on Bertha's pack, I headed for the garage, wheeled out my new bike, and climbed on. The minute I started pedaling up our driveway, I felt a little better. Soon I was speeding along, the wind whistling through my helmet. Much better! Turning off Clayton Road, I barreled down a slope, then shifted into an easier gear, pedaling furiously to get a start on the hill ahead. This bike was a dream! Coasting down the next hill, I shifted again, then remembered how the saleswoman at the bike shop said to pedal when I changed gears. I circled my feet, and heard a thunk as the bike chain snapped onto a new sprocket wheel.

I kept going, up hills and down, leaving my

problems far behind. When I came to the peak of the steepest hill, I rolled to a stop and walked my bike off the road.

This was a favorite spot of mine. The valley below was filled with high-rise apartment buildings. It had always fascinated me, so many families, so many lives, all stacked one on top of the other. I liked to sit there and imagine what it would be like to live in a penthouse, to ride in an elevator just to get home.

But on this afternoon my mind took a different track. In all those thousands of apartments, I knew there wasn't one eleven-year-old girl who'd just been dropped like a hot potato by her two best friends. Okay, even if Michael and Gayle were doing math like they'd said, would it have killed them to ask me to come over and study with them? Maybe they'd left me out because I had smelly bad breath, like Jason Johnson. I held my hand up to my mouth, exhaled, and quickly took a sniff. It didn't seem all that awful, but there had to be something wrong with me, or they wouldn't have deserted me, would they? Briefly, I toyed with the idea of always wearing the ratty jeans and T-shirt I had on at that moment, the way Miss Havisham wore her bride's dress, so I'd never forget the day my best friends jilted me.

Feeling very much alone, I took Bertha out and noticed that her yarn hair was coming unglued and her mouth was smudged. She looked as if she'd had a hard day, too.

"Things don't always work out," I told her. "Sometimes you want something very badly, but you don't get it." I thought about tomorrow's Student Council election. "Sometimes you don't want something at all, but that's what you get." I pictured the sink full of dirty dishes. Bertha looked quite sympathetic. "And sometimes," I concluded, "no one wants to kiss you."

Putting my first two fingers together and pretending that they were the lips of some anonymous boy, I puckered up and practiced kissing a few times—even though I thought it extremely unlikely that I'd even need to know how. Then I just sat there, wallowing, until I noticed the apartment buildings were casting long shadows and I knew I'd better get home to that sink before my mom did.

I stood up and brushed off the gravel dust, absently peering over the edge of the hill. Instantly, I cupped my hand over my mouth to stifle a gasp. Somebody was down there! On a little grassy knob just below me sat a *boy*! Had he been there this whole time? Had he heard me, I wondered, talking to my hard-boiled egg? Or seen me kissing my fingers?

I peeked down at him again. As far as I could tell from the back of his head, he wasn't anyone I knew, but I must have looked at him a few seconds too long, because suddenly he turned around, and I realized that there, staring right at me, was my mother's favorite patient!

SURPRISES

I scrambled back from the edge of the hill. I wanted
out of there, and fast! Stuffing in Bertha and shoul-
dering her pack, I flipped up my kickstand and
pushed off, shifting my bike into the most powerful
gear. But when I pushed down on the pedal, my
foot met with no resistance. The crank spun
around, throwing me off balance. I skidded on
the gravel and crashed. My bike landed on top
of me.

For a second, I just lay there with the rear wheel
spinning over my head, the bike chain hanging
limply on my knee. Nothing hurt. That was a good
sign. But my legs and the bike were so tangled up,
I couldn't tell what I had to do first to get up.

Then, before I knew what was happening, my bike was hoisted skyward. Scooting out from under it, I looked up and saw the boy. He held the seat of my bike with one hand and the handlebars with the other. On that hand, he wore a thick brown glove.

I struggled to my feet. "Thanks."

He lowered the bike to the ground. As I took it from him, he whisked his gloved hand away, hiding it behind his back.

Could he possibly recognize me from the awful picture on my mom's desk? I didn't think so, but I didn't want to stick around to find out.

"Well, uh, thanks." I started to push off again.

"Are you a total idiot?" he exclaimed.

Surprised, I stopped. I'd forgotten about my messed-up bike chain.

"What'd you do, change gears without pedaling?"

"I guess."

"Bet you can't walk and chew gum at the same time, either!" He laughed, meanly.

"It's a new bike," I told him. "I'm just not used to it yet." I looked down at the slack chain. Could I fix it, I wondered. Vaguely, I remembered the woman at the bike store explaining what to do if the chain slipped off, but I hadn't paid attention. I kicked at the chain. Was I going to have to walk my bike home? That would take at least an hour. I could feel the boy's eyes on me as I stood there, trying to figure out what to do.

All of a sudden, he grabbed the bike from me. Impatiently, he laid it on its side. "Hold it steady," he commanded.

I knelt down and held the bike frame. The gears were tilted up, facing the boy. He took the chain in his good hand and awkwardly tried to slip it over one of the rear sprocket wheels, but the chain seemed too short to reach around it.

"I'll have to walk it home," I said.

The boy glared at me angrily. Then he yanked off his glove, throwing it to the ground behind him.

Without thinking, I turned my face away, pretending to study the fascinating leaf patterns of a nearby bush.

"Don't worry," he said gruffly. "It's not contagious."

"So who's worried?"

"You. Scared to see a couple of blown-off fingers?"

"I am not." I turned and deliberately stared at his hand. From the wrist down, it was very white. Raised red scars crisscrossed his knuckles. There wasn't much left of his thumb or first finger, and his second finger was missing its tip. I wondered if his hand still hurt.

I watched as the boy struggled silently with my bike. He pulled the gear changer on the rear wheel toward him, and then, by trying the handlebar shifters in various positions, finally managed to line up the chain on one of the sprocket wheels. When he let go, the chain tightened into place.

"Hey, you did it!"

"Don't sound so surprised." He rotated the pedals a few times to make sure the chain was secure. "Or didn't you think the gimp could do it?" Standing up, he wiped the chain grease from his hands onto his jeans.

"If I didn't think you could do it, I would just have walked it home," I said, picking up my bike.

The boy shrugged. Frowning, he turned around, searching the ground with his eyes.

It took me a minute to figure out what he was looking for.

"There it is," I told him. "Under that bush."

He picked up his glove and slapped the dust off against his knee. "Your bike's fixed," he said, shoving his hand angrily into the glove. "So take off, moron!"

"I'm going!" I put my foot on the pedal, then turned around. "You don't have to be so mean!"

"You don't know anything!" he shouted at me.

"I know plenty!" I shouted back. "I know your hand looks a whole lot scarier when you put on that ugly old glove!"

"Get outta here, you four-eyes!" he yelled.

"You . . . you glove hand!" I screamed.

With that, I gave a mighty shove and sped off down the hill. My heart pounded wildly against my rib cage. How could I have said that? How could I? I didn't *do* things like that! What would my mom think if she found out I'd called him *glove hand*?

I pedaled for all I was worth, wishing and wishing that I could take back my words. Yank them back and swallow them! But I couldn't, ever. As I rode, I tried to calm myself, and think about what could have made me yell at him like that. He'd yelled at me, called me moron and four-eyes! He was so angry and mean! Was it just to me? It couldn't be. He didn't even know me. Maybe he was like that all the time, to everyone—to his parents, to his friends, if he had any . . . to my mom. And at that moment, I began to understand why she was so frustrated over this boy. He had problems, big problems, that went beyond his accident. She was trying to help him get better, but he'd be hard to help. I knew my mom would be ashamed of me if she found out what I'd called him, but I also knew that she hadn't spent her time thinking about this boy because she preferred him to me. Right now, I realized, he needed my mom's worrying a lot more than I did.

Almost without knowing how I'd gotten there, I found myself coasting down our driveway. I pulled my bike into the empty garage. With everything that had happened, I'd still beat my parents home.

Once in the kitchen, it hit me that in all the confusion, I hadn't even checked on Bertha! Half afraid to look, I zipped open the pack. Bertha sat as usual in her little seat, but across her cheek ran a jagged line. None of her white or yolk was sticking out, but my egg-baby was cracked.

A tear ran down my cheek and dropped onto Bertha's face, smearing her smile a bit more. It wasn't my fault that I'd fallen off my bike, was it? But it was. I should have remembered how to change gears. I wasn't a good parent. I'd let my baby get cracked, and even if I did miss out on Shell Shock, it wasn't going to uncrack her.

Still crying a little, I set Bertha gently in an eggcup on a shelf, turned on the faucet, and squirted detergent into the sink. I had so much to think about that I hardly noticed the sodden cereal. I'd broken Bertha. I'd called that boy an awful name. And I'd lost my two best friends. It was obvious that I had to change. But how? I racked my brain, and by the time I'd washed the dishes, I'd figured out a thing or two. I had to stop wallowing, for starters. Then, to prove I could make something besides mistakes, I'd make dinner. A meat loaf! I'd watched Gayle make one and it looked pretty simple. I imagined my hardworking mother opening the door and saying, "Mmmm! What smells so good?" I envisioned my dad taking a bite of my creation and saying, "This is just the way we used to cook 'em at Boy Scout camp!"

I put some frozen ground beef into the microwave, and while it was thawing, I took out all the little bottles from the fridge door. With meat loaf, I remembered Gayle saying, one can improvise! Into a mixing bowl I put a spoonful each of mayo, mustard, horseradish, Tabasco, oyster sauce, mint jelly, soy sauce, and tossed in a few capers, tiny onions, and green olives. Next, I picked up an egg to crack it, but it didn't seem right, so I put Bertha's distant relative back into the fridge. With all those other ingredients, no one would notice that this meat loaf didn't have an egg.

Luckily, Ms. Wong hadn't given us tomatoes to take care of, so I felt no remorse in pouring lots of ketchup into the bowl. I searched for bread crumbs, and then remembered that Gayle had finished them off, but in the cabinet over the sink I found a bag of turkey stuffing, which looked a lot like bread crumbs. I was about to shake it on top of the other ingredients, when a Great Idea suddenly stirred itself into my head.

I was nervous about the meat loaf, it being my first one and all. I carried it to the table on a platter.

My dad took a sniff. "Do I detect another of Gayle's surprises?"

"Nope," I told him. "It's my meat loaf."

"Well, well." He helped himself to the green beans.

"I'm sure it'll be fine, Lila," said my mom as she sliced into my creation, "but if it turns out that we want anything else, I've got a couple things in the freezer."

"Hey, wait a second!" I objected. "You think it's going to be awful!"

"Oh, don't be so sensitive, Lila," my mom said

in a tired voice. "Not everything turns out to be a masterpiece when you're just learning to cook."

"But you haven't even tried it!"

Without any more talk, my mom and dad both took bites. They chewed in silence for what seemed a long time. My dad spoke first. "Very tasty, Lila. Definitely up to Camp Ironvale standards!"

I took a bite myself. Maybe it was a little less spicy than Gayle's had been, but it wasn't half bad.

After dinner, my mom stirred her tea and said, "It was a wonderful meal, honey!"

"Really?"

"Really. I'm sorry I had doubts. It's just that you've never shown any interest in cooking before, and I was afraid maybe you'd been struck by some wild idea and used"—she smiled and shrugged— "well, who knows what in the meat loaf."

"But I did get a Great Idea," I said.

"Now that I've eaten it, I'm almost afraid to ask," said my mom, "but what *did* you use?"

I grinned over at her. "A cookbook."

GAYLE
FOR PRESIDENT!

On Friday morning, I left for school early to show Bertha's injury to Dr. Wong. My fate as a Shell Shock fan was in her hands.

"Hmmm," she mused, turning my egg-baby over. "It's a fracture, all right."

"Is it serious?"

"Bertha's scarred, but she'll survive." Dr. Wong put the tiniest-size Band-Aid across Bertha's cheek and gave her back to me. "You can stay in the eggsperiment."

"Thanks, Dr. Wong!" I wished I could hug Bertha, but I didn't want to cause any more cracks. I thanked my lucky stars that I wasn't going to miss out on the concert!

Ms. Wong said she was on her way to our classroom, so we walked down the hallway together.
She didn't start chatting, and I was glad. I hadn't
spoken to Gayle since I'd left her standing with
Michael, and I needed a few minutes to go over
the plan I'd made for what I was going to say to
her. I was so busy mentally rehearsing that when
we got to the sixth-grade door I thought I'd walked
into the wrong room! Standing up front where
Sandra usually conducted the class meetings was
Roger Rupp's mother holding Roger's baby
brother.

"Here's Ms. Wong now," said Mr. Sherman.
"You're late, Ms. Fenwick."

I slid into my desk and looked around. Everyone
else seemed as confused as I felt. Everyone except
Roger. He was slumped down in his desk as if he
wished he could disappear.

"I believe most of you know Mrs. Rupp," said
Ms. Wong, walking to where Roger's mother was
standing, "and Frankie."

"Da! Da!" Frankie crowed happily at the sound
of his name.

"Hey, Frankie speaks Russian!" Michael called
out.

Roger's brother was dressed in a fuzzy blue suit
with feet. His dark hair stuck straight up on the
top of his head like a punk rocker's, and he had
two little teeth poking up on the bottom of an
otherwise gummy grin.

"I invited Mrs. Rupp and Frankie to come today
to help you with your last assignment, which is to

write in your books about the differences between caring for an egg-baby and for a real baby." Ms. Wong gave Roger's mother a go-ahead nod.

"Well, Frankie is almost seven months old now," began Mrs. Rupp. "He's cutting teeth, and it makes his gums feel good when he chews on things."

As if to demonstrate, Frankie stuck his whole fist into his mouth and gummed it happily.

"His favorite game right now is peek-a-boo." Mrs. Rupp carried Frankie over to Kelly. "Want to try it?"

Kelly looked Frankie in the eye. The baby squirmed with happiness. Then she put her hands over her face and right away Frankie's smile faded. He looked kind of worried. But when Kelly swung her hands away from her face and said, "Peek-a-boo!" Frankie looked really surprised and then started laughing like a maniac.

Mrs. Rupp carried Frankie around to a few other kids and let them try peeking and booing.

"Doesn't he know there's a face behind the hands?" asked Eddie.

"Yeah," chimed in Barney. "Are babies stupid?"

"No," said Mrs. Rupp. "They're just babies. Frankie's mind hasn't developed enough to let him figure out peek-a-boo, but it will. Playing games like this over and over helps babies learn about the world."

After a couple more rounds, Frankie buried his head in his mother's neck and refused to look at anyone.

"It's not that hard, taking care of a baby, is it?"

Rita asked. "I mean, don't they just, like, sleep most of the time?"

Mrs. Rupp laughed. "That's what I thought before Roger was born."

"Mom!" moaned Roger.

"But I was wrong. Babies keep you busier than you can imagine. When I want to go out, I have to make sure Frankie has on a clean diaper, dress him, and pack up a bag with some juice."

Frankie started making uh-uh-uh fussing noises, so Mrs. Rupp put him down on the floor, where he happily tried to scoot around on his belly.

"And sometimes, when I'm ready to go out the door, I realize that Frankie needs changing again, so it's back to square one!"

Now she sounded like my mom.

"It's hard work, but it's very rewarding to love babies and to watch them grow and . . . oh, dear!"

We all followed Mrs. Rupp's gaze down to Frankie, who was gnawing on a leg of Mr. Sherman's desk.

"You can't take your eyes off a baby for a second!" Mrs. Rupp scooped him up and tried to wipe off his tongue. Frankie took this opportunity to try out his new teeth.

"Ow! Frankie!" Mrs. Rupp cried, wrenching her finger loose.

"Hey, it's a vampire baby!" yelled Barney.

Deprived of the desk leg and his mother's finger, Frankie shut his eyes and began to howl.

"I think we'll go now," shouted Mrs. Rupp over the baby's wails.

"Thank you for coming," Ms. Wong yelled back.
"Thank you, Mrs. Rupp!" we all called out.
"Bye, Frankie!"

The door to our classroom closed behind the crying baby and for a few seconds no one said anything. I think we all appreciated the quiet.

Finally, Barney asked Roger, "Is Frankie always that loud?"

"That was nothing," scoffed Roger. "You should hear him when you try to get him to stop hugging the dog."

Because of Frankie's visit, we had to work extra-furiously that morning, so I didn't get a chance to say a word to Gayle in the classroom. My plan was just to start talking, tell her all about the boy with the glove and about my meat loaf, but never mention the thing with Michael. Cool as a cucumber, I'd simply pretend that it had never happened.

At recess, I cornered her by the jungle gym. "What's with you and Michael, anyway?" I burst out. "I have never felt so rejected in my entire life!"

So much for the cool approach.

"Just homework, Lila."

"No, it wasn't. You like Michael now, don't you?"

Gayle looked down at her shoes, her good ones because of the Student Council speech. "I've always liked Michael."

"But I mean *like* like, like love."

Gayle laughed. "You sound like Rita with all those 'likes.' " She put Albert E.'s shoe box on the ground beside the jungle gym and grabbed a bar with one hand, swinging herself slowly back and forth. "I don't know," she said at last. "I like being with him. He's smart and he makes me laugh a lot, so I thought maybe I did like him, but it's hard to explain."

"Did you kiss him?"

"Lila!"

"Well, did you?"

"Forget it!" Gayle was quiet for a few seconds, thinking, and then said, "It's mental."

"What's mental?"

"The way I like Michael. I like the way he thinks, I like the way his mind works."

"What you're saying is that you just like his *brain*?"

Gayle nodded. "Right. No Romeo and Juliet, no true love, no fireworks."

"Fireworks?" Now I knew for sure I'd never understand this boy-girl stuff.

"Anyway," Gayle was saying, "I wanted to be with him, by ourselves, to see what it felt like. It just sort of happened after school, so there wasn't time to explain it to you, but I'm sorry I hurt your feelings."

"I was in a bad mood, anyway. I just didn't want to lose my best friend on top of everything else that had gone wrong."

"Listen," Gayle said almost sternly, "even if I

do like some boy someday, which I may or may not, I won't let it change anything between us. Not ever again."

"But you'll want to be with him instead of me."

Gayle shook her head. "You're my best friend. We've got history together! Think of everything we've been through. Remember the sleep-over when we ordered the kitchen-sink pizza? That was the same night we watched the old version of *Invasion of the Body Snatchers*. You went bonkers when those pod people started showing up!"

As Gayle spoke, it was almost like being hypnotized again. Good old, bad old, funny old times came back inside my head.

"And remember how scared you were when you broke that window at Weekeegan Lodge?"

I remembered.

"And what about our spaghetti fight? And the time we camped out in your back yard?" Gayle started giggling. "When that cat walked into the tent, you screamed bloody murder!"

"And you laughed so hard you wet your pants!"

That cracked Gayle up. We stood there by the jungle gym, laughing like crazy. She sobered up first and gave me a mock-angry glare. "And then there was slimeade!"

"Guess that wasn't the world's Greatest Idea, huh?"

"In time my trifling pain shall fade," Gayle said. She picked up Albert E.'s shoe box and grabbed me by the elbow as the bell rang. "But the flower of our friendship? Never!" Arm in arm, we marched up the school steps, best friends forever.

All that morning, I felt so good. It was Gayle and me, together again. Not even a page of long-division problems took my happiness away. As I worked, I tried to think of some way that I could show Gayle how glad I was that we were best friends, and maybe, somehow, give her Student Council campaign a little boost. By the time I'd finished the last problem, I'd figured out a way. I didn't have much time—just lunch hour—but I did have a Great Idea. The only hitch was that it depended entirely on whether I could talk Mrs. Goldstein into letting me use the school's copy machine.

Right after lunch, all Price Schoolers, grades one and up, filed into what on assembly days is called the auditorium but is otherwise known as the gym. I managed to find an inconspicuous spot by the door, and since Mrs. Goldstein had cooperated, I handed all the sixth-grade girls a sheet of paper as they entered. For the short time that I'd had to work on this idea, I felt that it had turned out pretty well.

"Attention!" Mrs. Alexander, the principal, stood behind the podium on the stage at the far end of the room. "Boys and girls! Please quiet down, so that we may begin the assembly!"

Behind her, sitting stiffly on folding chairs arranged in a semicircle, were the eight candidates.

Gayle, Eddie, and Kelly had their shoe boxes under their chairs, and Rita held her basket on her lap.

"Thank you, boys and girls," said Mrs. Alexander, when at last the noise in the gym subsided. "We are here today to hear what the candidates for the Student Council offices of treasurer, secretary, vice president, and president have to say. Listen carefully, because when they are finished, you will go back to your classrooms and vote for one student for each office."

Mrs. Alexander nodded to Tim, who sat in the first chair on the left of the stage. Tim walked up to where Mrs. Alexander had been standing, but he was so short that we couldn't even see the top of his head until she moved the podium away.

"My name is Tim Petefish and I am running for treasurer of Student Council," Tim read in a wavery voice from a piece of notebook paper which trembled in his hands. "I like math and could add and subtract the Student Council's money. I think I would do a good job. Thank you."

We all gave Tim a hand. He was followed by Zoe Rupp, who was also running for treasurer, and then by another fifth-grader, Warren Hardy, who was running for secretary. Everyone gave the usual short, formal speeches, until it was Rita's turn. She sauntered to center stage and began by telling the audience how absolutely thrilled she was to be there. She talked about her excellent handwriting and how she could take notes practically better than a tape recorder. She went on for so long that Mrs. Alexander finally started tapping her watch, but Rita just talked faster and finally finished up by saying that she had the world's cutest stationery all picked out, with pink scratch-and-sniff roses on it, for writing the Student Council thank-you notes.

Kelly and Justin Susman went next, giving their speeches for the vice-presidential spot, and finally, because Deckert comes before English in the alphabet, it was Gayle's turn.

I glanced over at Lynn and Sandra. They gave me a nod. All the other sixth-grade girls were holding the papers I'd given them, too. We were ready!

"Mrs. Alexander, teachers, and fellow students," Gayle began, "I am here today to tell you my qualifications for the office of Student Council president."

Gazing at Gayle, I was struck by how serious she looked up there, serious and capable and grownup. My best friend was an impressive person! Not only did she look good, but as I listened to her speech, I realized that her ideas were first-rate, too. She talked about a recycling project to save notebook paper, and how the Student Council might earn money by installing a juice machine in the cafeteria. As she spoke, a feeling of dread crept into the pit of my stomach. Operation Girl Power, Operation Slimeade . . . Would Operation Sing-Along join those other two as a miserable flop?

As the last words of Gayle's speech died away in the gym, I tried to signal to Sandra to forget what we'd planned, but all the sixth-grade girls were already on their feet. Shakily, I stood up with them. Holding our papers, we began singing to the tune of the "Battle Hymn of the Republic":

> *Our eyes will see the glory of Gayle for president!*
> *To beat her in this election would be harder than cement!*
> *She will lead Price School to honor!*
> *She will never, never fail!*
> *The truth is—WE WANT GAYLE!*

I dared to look up when we'd finished the verse. Gayle was smiling. I waved my hands like an orchestra leader and encouraged all the kids in the school to join in on the chorus:

> *Gayle, Gayle, Gayle Deckert!*
> *Gayle, Gayle, Gayle Deckert!*
> *Gayle, Gayle, Gayle Deckert!*
> *Gayle for president!*

Wild applause broke out in the gym as we girls sat down, and then, as if it had been part of the plan, Rob Boxer and a group of fifth-graders popped up and started singing the same tune, but a very different verse. I watched in horror as kids in every grade stood up and joined in the singing.

Mine eyes have seen the glory of the burning
  of the school!
We have tortured every teacher!
We have broken every rule!
We are marching down the hallway now, to
  hang the pincipool!
As the school comes tumbling down!

After the "Glory, glory, hallelujahs," and huge burst of cheering, Mrs. Alexander managed to silence everyone by turning off the lights in the gym and holding up two fingers, which is her "quiet sign."

Gayle was staring down into her lap, so her hair hid her face, but it looked as if she was trying with all her might not to laugh.

Poor Eddie! He walked to the front of the stage and gave his speech, about his experience as Student Council vice president and how hard he'd work, but no one really seemed to be listening. When he finished, we were dismissed.

Back in the sixth-grade room, Mr. Sherman never said a word about the near-riot we'd incited with our song. I think he knew we'd just been trying to help Gayle and hadn't suspected what would result. He simply conducted the class vote as though nothing unusual had happened.

Right before school ended, Mrs. Goldstein came into our room and handed Mr. Sherman an envelope with the election results. He picked up his scissors and slit it open.

"You look like you're about to present an Academy Award, Mr. Sherman," Kelly told him.

He smiled but didn't take the paper out of the envelope. "All of you who ran for office did an excellent job of preparing your speeches and presenting them today. Only one person can be elected to each office, it's true, but those of you who are not the victors should still feel good about running a fine race."

I crossed my fingers, hoping that Gayle would win. If she lost, I knew I'd be to blame.

Mr. Sherman cleared his throat. "This year's Student Council treasurer will be Tim Petefish."

"All right!" shouted Barney.

"The secretary will be Warren Hardy."

Rita put her head down on her desk.

"Vice president will be Kelly MacConnell."

Please, please, please! I crossed another pair of fingers.

"President will be Gayle Deckert."

I let out the breath I'd been holding and leaped over to Gayle. "You did it! You won!"

After I hugged my best friend, I looked over to see how Eddie was taking the first defeat of his life, and saw Rita draped over his desk. "I know *exactly* how you feel," she was saying.

When school let out, everyone came up to Gayle to congratulate her, so it was hard to get a word in edgewise. But I waited, and finally just the two of us were left on the sidewalk.

"How come you didn't tell me what you were

going to talk about in your speech?" I asked as we started walking toward Marky's Ice Cream Parlor, where I'd offered to treat us to double-dip victory cones. "That recycling project is really a good idea."

"Don't you think," said Gayle, "that maybe it's even a Great Idea?"

I thought about it for a minute. "It is. I guess I don't have a monopoly on Great Ideas."

Gayle grinned at my admission and then made one of her own. "Well, as my campaign manager, you certainly gave me a lot of voter recognition. Between slimeade and that song of yours, I don't think there's a single student in the whole school who doesn't know the name Gayle Deckert."

I had to agree. As I opened the door to Marky's, I turned to her. "You think being president of Student Council will be very hard?"

Gayle giggled. "Oh, no harder than cement!"

OVER EASY

"An egg-baby doesn't wake up in the middle of the night," Kelly read aloud from her egg-baby book. "When my aunt and uncle came to visit us, my baby cousin David slept in my room with me, and he woke up two or three times every night. Even though I really love him, I was sort of glad when he went home."

"Thank you, Kelly," Ms. Wong said. "Who's next?"

"Egg-babies and human babies actually have very little in common," read Michael. His spaceship home hung over to one side of his head today, as if the spring which attached it to his bike helmet was wearing out. "We think having to carry the eggs around with us everywhere is inconvenient, but it's easy compared to what it's like to be responsible for a real human baby."

Ms. Wong beamed at Michael.

"On the other hand," he went on, "the satisfactions that come from raising human babies are missing in caring for an egg-baby. Real babies learn to make sounds and finally to talk. They learn to crawl and walk. They smile at you and love you back.

"In conclusion, I believe that parents who understand what a big responsibility a baby is will be happier and have happier babies than parents who don't consider beforehand how much work it takes."

That was an A+ report if ever there was one!

"Thank you, Michael." Ms. Wong looked around the room. "That's everyone, isn't it?"

All of us who still had egg-babies nodded.

"I think we'll end the eggsperiment today instead of waiting until Friday," she announced. "I know all of you worked very hard, and even if your egg didn't survive, I hope this project encouraged you to think about big responsibilities, such as having a family, that you may face in the not-so-distant future."

No one had anything to say after that! Finally, Eddie broke the silence by asking what we should do with our eggs.

"What would you like to do with them?" asked Ms. Wong.

"I'll be happy not to carry Stan the Man around all the time," admitted Eddie, "but it doesn't seem right just to throw him out."

We all nodded.

Ms. Wong waited.

Lynn raised her hand. "Maybe we could put the egg-babies and their homes in the lobby display case."

Ms. Wong smiled. "I think the eggs will last a little longer without spoiling." She appointed Lynn head of a committee to arrange the display.

"Great idea," Kelly whispered to Lynn.

So Gayle wasn't the only one whose turn it was to come up with Great Ideas. Now Lynn had thought of one. Barney Barker'd probably get one next, and if everyone could come up with Great Ideas, then who'd need Lila Fenwick?

"Now," said Ms. Wong, "those of you who finished the eggsperiment please stay after library period for a moment so that I can give you some instructions. The rest of you are dismissed."

Fourteen of us remained in the library. We could hardly wait for Ms. Wong to hand out our Shell Shock tickets!

"Before you leave the library," Ms. Wong was saying, "please stack your egg-baby books on the table. I know the fourth- and fifth-graders are very interested in reading them." She looked at me. "And one first-grader has been asking me about them, too."

Gloria!

"And now," Ms. Wong went on, "here's the

news you've been waiting for. Since you have proven that you're responsible caretakers, Mr. Sherman has arranged to let you take care of some real live babies."

For a couple of seconds, we were too shocked to say a word.

"What?" Rita shrieked at last. *"That's* our reward? We get to baby-sit?"

Ms. Wong nodded.

"But . . . but . . . but . . ." Rita sounded like a motorboat.

"Rita thought the reward was tickets to the Shell Shock concert," explained Kelly.

"She did?" Ms. Wong's eyebrows went up. "I guess the rest of Mr. Sherman's idea won't come as a total surprise, then." She winked. "Rita's right. This Saturday, all of you are invited to the Fall Festival to look after some babies from the Downtown Day-Care Center. Their parents have been given tickets to the six-o'clock Shell Shock concert . . ."

"Their *parents*?" wailed Rita. "But what about *us*?"

"I was just getting to that, Rita. To thank you for volunteering to care for the children, the Festival has agreed to provide each of you with a ticket to the second concert."

Rita burst into tears and threw her arms around a startled Ms. Wong. Then we all began jumping up and down and hugging each other. We were really going to see Shell Shock!

Right after library period, Rita figured out that

there were 127 hours until the concert. She made herself a chart with 127 squares and colored them in with pastel markers as the hours went by.

Rita was just filling in her ninety-seventh square the next Friday afternoon when Mr. Sherman took *The Enormous Egg*, by Oliver Butterworth, from between the bookends on his desk. The new book we were listening to was about a boy who finds an egg that hatches into a dinosaur. We all liked the story a lot, but every time Mr. Sherman opened the book, Tim and Roger were practically on the edges of their seats! Today Mr. Sherman hadn't even finished the first sentence when Ms. Wong peeked in our door.

"Would this be a good time to make an announcement?" she asked.

"A fine time," Mr. Sherman said. Even though he didn't allow any other interruptions in his classroom, Mr. Sherman certainly never seemed to mind Ms. Wong's popping in.

"The staff of the Price School paper will have its first meeting next Monday," Ms. Wong said.

The paper! I'd forgotten about my stupid interview! If only I'd tried to make a serious list so that I could have been a reporter.

"I wish all of you could be on the staff," Ms. Wong was saying, "but everyone is invited to write articles and stories and submit them to the editor in chief." She pulled out a list. "The following students will be the first staff. Eddie English, Sandra Guth, Rita Morgan, Barbara Fox, and Lynn Williamson."

I felt like putting my head down on my desk, the way Rita had done when she'd lost her Student Council election, but I didn't. I stared bravely at Chocolate nibbling away on a lettuce leaf in her cage.

"The editor in chief," Ms. Wong was saying, "will have the overall responsibility for the paper."

I knew she'd pick Michael, no contest.

"Now, a good editor in chief needs unique qualifications. Curiosity is important, and so are stick-to-it-iveness and the ability to organize things. Perhaps the most important is the willingness to go to great lengths to get a good story. And I'll bet we're going to be reading some fascinating interviews with this student in charge."

I had my hands all set to clap for Michael when I heard Ms. Wong say, "Lila Fenwick."

For a minute, I thought I'd missed something. Was she asking me a question? But when everyone started coming up and pounding me on the back, I finally figured out that she was appointing me, Lila Fenwick, editor in chief of the paper!

As I sat there in my glory, it occurred to me that if awful things can happen in a split second, well, so can wonderful things; very wonderful things, indeed.

After Ms. Wong left, Mr. Sherman started reading *The Enormous Egg* again, but I didn't hear a word. My mind was whirling with things that could go into that first issue. I'd ask Mr. Sherman if I could borrow *The Enormous Egg* over the weekend to read this chapter to myself. Somehow, I knew he'd understand. And even though he was reading us another book now, suddenly it felt as if *Great Expectations* might not be over after all!

When we sat down to dinner that night, I waited to give my parents my good news. I wanted to tell it just the right way at just the right moment.

My mom set a cheesy eggplant casserole on the table, which probably meant that she was heading into another one of her vegetarian phases, but today I didn't even mind. She seemed particularly cheerful this evening as she dished out her glop. My dad noticed it, too. "You look like the cat that swallowed the canary, Fran."

She laughed. "I'm not sure if I'd put it that way, but, yes, I am feeling good. You know the boy who had the firecracker accident?"

For a split second, fear seized me. I'd sworn Gayle to secrecy when I'd told her about the boy, but what if her mom had pried it out of her? And what if her mom had told my mom? Told how I'd called him *glove hand*! Then I realized that if my mom knew, she would not be one bit cheerful.

"Well, it may not sound like all that much progress to you, Phil, but today he held a pen in his right hand and wrote a few lines. He didn't take his glove off, not yet, but just the fact that he was willing to try using his injured hand is a big breakthrough."

Part of me wanted to tell my mom what had happened up there on that hill; how her favorite patient had tossed off his glove and used his injured hand very effectively. But the wiser part said no. If I told her that, everything would come pouring out. Instead, I said, "I've got some good news, too. Guess who the editor in chief of the new school paper is going to be?"

If they'd guessed Gayle, I would have dumped my eggplant on their heads.

My dad whistled. "Editor in chief! That's a powerful position."

"Congratulations, honey!" said my mom. "You know, I've always thought you had the makings of a great journalist."

I told them how Ms. Wong wanted to call the paper *Price in Print*, but how I was still holding out for *The Priceless Press*, and about who else was on the staff, and some ideas I had for stories. "And," I finished up, "I'm going to save space in every issue for interviews, not just with the kids who run everything, but with the less noticeable kids. I bet they'll have lots of interesting things to say."

I could tell they both thought that was a Great Idea.

In spite of predictions for rain, Saturday turned out to be blue-skied and breezy. A *Priceless Press*

weather headline might have read: "Fabulously
Fair for Fall Festival." We fourteen eggsperts, as
Ms. Wong called us, met at school at three o'clock,
and a minibus took us downtown.

There, around the Gateway Arch, beside the
muddy Mississippi River, thousands of people
milled about among booths selling everything from
frog puppets that stuck their tongues out when
you squeezed a little bulb to french-fried frog legs.
Yuck!

We walked around in a group with Mr. Sherman, Ms. Wong, and Ms. Sherry for a while. Then
Rita talked Gayle, Kelly, Lynn, and me into dress-
ing up in these old-fashioned clothes from the sixties and having our pictures taken as hippies. She
even bought us each a copy with the money she'd
made from Humpty Dumpty's Baby Basket! When
we showed the photograph to Mr. Sherman, he
said the word "old-fashioned" did not yet apply
to the sixties!

Barney, Michael, and Eddie spent most of their
money at a booth where they banged this huge
wooden hammer down really hard and tried to
send a little metal disk up a pole to ring a bell.
Funny phrases were written all the way to the top.
On his last turn, Barney hit the disk up to TOP DOG.
The best Eddie got was SAD SACK, but in our books
he was still a TKO. And believe it or not, Michael
and his muscles actually rang the bell! For a prize,
he got a hairy orange stuffed dog. He held it out
to Gayle, but she said it was gross and wouldn't

take it. Then Rita piped up and said she'd *love* to have the doggie, which she promptly named Nigel, after her current Shell Shock favorite. Gayle whispered to me that she didn't think she even liked Michael's brain anymore.

By the time we left the bell-ringing booth, a long line had formed behind it, and right in the middle of the line I spotted the last person in the world I wanted to see.

"Oh, no!" I ducked behind Gayle.

"Lila, what's wrong?"

"Just keep walking," I whispered. "He's here, the boy with the glove!"

Gayle stopped. "Where?"

"Keep moving!"

"I don't see anyone with a glove."

I peeked out from behind Gayle's shoulder. There he was, standing next to a dark-haired girl who seemed to be laughing at something he'd said. I noticed that he was laughing, too. And then I noticed his hand. His right hand. He wasn't wearing any glove.

When we were a safe distance away, I pointed him out to Gayle.

"Very TKO," she whispered. "And his hand doesn't look all that bad."

Gayle was right. Old Glove Hand must have had his glove off and been out in the sunlight quite a bit since I'd seen him. My guess was that when he was good and ready one day, he'd whip off his glove and show my mom that he could do everything she hoped—and a whole lot more—with his injured hand. At that moment I felt a pang of sympathy for my unsuspecting mother.

At five o'clock, we walked over to the concert area where Shell Shock was warming up. When Rita got within ten feet of the stage and spotted Boris's gong-and-drum set, she went into some kind of a trance and tilted her sickening chartreuse snow cone so far over that it dribbled down her leg and onto her sock.

Mr. Sherman found the director of the Downtown Day-Care Center, and she led us to a big green-and-white-striped tent, where the babies were waiting.

Each of us was paired with parents and a baby, except for Rita. She was assigned to the only mother with twins! Some of the moms and dads didn't really look old enough to have children, but there they were, with real live babies to take care of.

Of course, our teachers stayed with us to make sure everything went smoothly. We talked with the parents for about half an hour before the concert began, and they gave us instructions about bottles and burping and patty-cake. It didn't take long for the babies to get comfortable with us.

My baby's name was Vanessa. She was round-faced and curly-headed, and just a little older than Roger's brother, but she could crawl, and fast! Her fat little knees were all grass-stained. I fell in love with her the minute I saw her, and thought what a Great Idea it would be to start doing some regular baby-sitting.

When Shell Shock turned the amplifiers up, the moms and dads headed for their seats. Only the twins started crying when their mother left. The rest of the babies seemed to think hanging out with us was going to be just fine.

Vanessa's idea of a good time was to crawl, at about fifty miles an hour, to the tent entrance. There, I'd scoop her up, she'd shriek with delight, and I'd carry her back to the middle of the tent, where she'd zoom off for the entrance again. It was aerobic exercise just chasing after her!

Gayle got a sleeping infant, so all she had to do was sit on the grass and hold the baby.

Michael wasn't so lucky. He was looking after a two-year-old named Joshua. Not five minutes after his mother left, Joshua started stinking something awful and Michael had to change a whopper of a diaper. Ms. Wong helped him, and he acted like it was no big deal, but I could tell he was breathing through his mouth the whole time!

Barney's baby, Kayla, bapped him on the head a couple of times with her stuffed giraffe, but then he scooped her up and put her on his knee.

> *Little baby Kayla-koo*
> *Bounces like a kangaroo!*

For the rest of their time together, Kayla planted big wet kisses on Barney and shrieked, "More bounce!"

The twins gave Rita a real runaround. Margie was a notorious biter. When she'd toddle up to any of the other babies, they'd run off, crying. Stuart's favorite trick was to grab other children's toys, pile them up, and sit on them. Rita had to beg Ms. Sherry to help her watch the two babies. Before the first concert was even over, Margie had yanked the rubber band out of Rita's ponytail and Stuart had spit up on her purse. "Really," she told me, as the faint strains of Shell Shock's closing number reached our ears, "it isn't safe for people to have twins!"

The moms and dads took their time showing up after the concert. I guessed they didn't get many offers of free nighttime sitting and they wanted to make the most of it. When they finally came into the tent, we all hugged and kissed our babies good-bye and hurried off. We had only about ten minutes to buy hot dogs and drinks before the second concert was to begin.

Gayle and I were the last ones to follow Mr. Sherman to our seats. They were great ones, too, in the fifth and sixth rows! Rita just about knocked poor Lynn over so she could sit in the fifth row by Eddie! I looked around for two seats next to each other so that Gayle and I could sit together. I didn't see any seats, but I saw Michael tilting his head toward the empty seat next to his in the sixth row. "Hey, Fenwick!" he called. "This chair's got your name on it!"

I hesitated. Normally, I wouldn't have thought

anything about my old friend saving me a seat. But now, with all the Gayle-and-Michael mess about who-liked-who, I wasn't so sure.

"Go on." Gayle gave me a little shove.

I looked back at her. "But there's only one seat."

"It's okay." Gayle pointed to Kelly, who was sitting sprawled out on two chairs and waving her over. "Talk to you at intermission."

So I went and sat down by Michael, and even though I'd been good friends with him since my own diaper days, this felt different. Michael didn't look at me cross-eyed or crack any jokes, the way he usually did. He just sat there, staring straight ahead, and so that's what I did, too. What was going on? And then the lights went down and suddenly the sky above the arch exploded in a kaleidoscope of fireworks. Giant pinwheels crackled over our heads, giving off a flickering pink glow. I looked at Michael and he was looking at me, and we both started laughing, and that's when I figured out that Michael didn't have any more idea than I did about what was going on.

With a low whistle, a dozen little spheres of white fire zigzagged their way up into the sky, where they burst in a cluster of heart-stopping booms. Everyone screamed and Shell Shock ran onto the stage. In the circling spotlights, Boris slammed his head on his gong a couple times while Oggie grabbed a mike and began belting out, "Oooo, I can't keep up with you, baby!"

"I should have sung that to Vanessa!" I shouted to Michael over the ultra-loud sound.

We sat there then, beneath the starry sky, and experienced Shell Shock rock. During the second number, I noticed that Rita was leaning over toward Eddie. By the middle of the next song, her head was actually resting on his shoulder! Michael elbowed me. He'd noticed it, too. Eddie must have felt us staring, because after a minute he slowly turned his head around and kind of shrugged, and that's when I realized that, three songs into the concert, Rita Morgan, baby-sitter of twins and Shell Shock fan supreme, had fallen sound asleep.